BAD BOY

J.C. REED

&

JACKIE STEELE

An Indecent Proposal: Bad Boy

Copyright © 2016 J.C. Reed & Jackie Steele

All rights reserved.

Cover art by Larissa Klein

Editing by Shannon Wolfman

Inline Editing by Kim Bias

ISBN: 1522898220
ISBN-13: 978-1522898221

BAD BOY

I should have seen it coming.

Sexy? Handsome? Trouble? Check, check, and check.

Is he messing up my life? Hell yes.

All the signs are there: he is a bad boy.

Even his name is a lie. Too bad I married him. I can't wait to get divorced. Does this make me sound crazy?

I know I should avoid him, run as fast as I can. However, when a harmless misunderstanding lands me in a foreign prison cell, my dear, lying husband is the only one who can get me out. Crap. I shouldn't accept.

But how to say no to trouble when said trouble is the one who makes me fantasize all the dirty things he could do to me?

Chapter 1

WHY IS IT always that the moment you've let a guy into your heart—or panties, for that matter—he turns into a big, ugly frog?

Or a jerk.

Or a lying bastard, who'd do anything to keep manipulating you so you fall for whatever agenda he's going for. A hidden motive that made him want to fuck with your mind in the first place.

Less than twenty-four hours ago, I had married a man I knew nothing about.

A stranger.

An enigma with more layers to him than I cared to admit, because my intelligence refused to let me

3

acknowledge the fact that I had been fooled by gray blue eyes and a hard body that belonged on a men's health magazine; not to mention a tongue that knew how to fill me and lick me until I panted his name. Or maybe it was his deep, sexy voice, able to arouse me with sweet words of nothingness, that had made me lose my sanity.

Exactly those sweet words of nothingness and hot bundles of defined muscles, as my best friend Jude liked to call them, had pushed me into more than just his bed.

They got me married—fake married—to an even faker jerk with a fake name.

They got me completely screwed.

Those were the kind of dark thoughts running through my mind as I stepped out of the airport in Acapulco and into the blazing heat, a huge tee shirt and black shades shielding me from the afternoon sun that did nothing to improve my mood.

My two, brand-new suitcases were filled with dresses, shoes, and books—anything the shop assistant thought I would need for my trip. A "recovery trip" she'd called it when she saw my unshed tears and found out I had booked a plane to Mexico. She'd instantly assumed I was running from a bad break up. A bad breakup was theoretically correct, though the guy did not do the dumping.

I broke up in writing, like the coward I was, or used to be, right before I ran away from him, and now I was more than ready to embark on my next adventure in a quest to forget him.

Because, to be honest, I was sick of my mascara-smeared face.

I was sick of guys with blue eyes that could melt your heart.

Sick of being the pushover of a guy who thought he owned the world.

Who the hell did he think he was?

Thor?

Just because he so happened to be perfect: tall, handsome, and tanned, with a smile that melted your reserve, didn't mean he could get away with whatever the hell he wanted.

Maybe he was Loki—Thor's evil and hot brother. He sure could lie just as well.

I pushed my glasses higher on my nose and plastered a fake smile on my face. I wouldn't let some god-faced idiot ruin my life just because my wits left me the moment he pulled off his shirt. Or because I gave him my V-card. And most certainly not because I soaked up all his I-care-for-you bullshit, like some stray puppy, while trying to maintain my dignity by playing hard to get.

Seriously, who had invented the notion of playing hard to get?

It got me nothing but trouble.

Call it my ego, my feelings being hurt. Call it even obsessive. But I couldn't stop checking my phone, even though it was switched off.

Holy shit.

It was hot in Mexico.

I paused to take shallow breaths and raised my head to feel the warm rays of sun on my face. I pushed the image of ocean blue eyes on a cloudy day and dark hair out of my mind, and focused on the narrow strip of blue stretching in the distance. I couldn't wait to slip into a bikini and hit the beach with a good book, ready to forget the world around me. Suddenly I couldn't wait to get to the hotel.

"Taxi." I stopped a tourist cab before it could drive off. "Habla inglés?" I asked the driver, a man in his fifties with a mustache. His head was cleanly shaven. His shirt looked like it had seen better days.

He looked from me to my suitcases, then nodded. "Un poquito. Where do you want to go?"

Sweat trickled down my back as I took my time checking the license on the right window, the taxi number plate to see if it was an official cab. The last thing I needed was to get into a pirated one, or worse yet, be kidnapped and held for ransom. But the taxi looked as official as they came.

I handed him a piece of paper with the address of the hotel and what I would be willing to pay for the drive, mentally thanking the shop assistant for her advice to settle for a price before getting into any taxi in Mexico.

The driver looked the paper over, then nodded again. "Muy bien, pero le advierto que ahora mismo hay mucho tráfico por allí." When he saw my confused expression, he explained. "Lots of traffic here, but I take a shortcut."

Shortcut?

The old me would have said no.

It was safe to say she would not have traveled to Mexico at all.

But the new me?

Gone were the days of being pushed around. I wanted to take charge, to discover and find myself.

"Sure," I said brightly, ignoring the pang of uneasiness settling in the pit of my stomach.

I just hoped his shortcut didn't involve a drive through all the areas that were frequented by the drug cartels.

That could really happen.

"Gracias." I slumped into the backseat, then leaned back exhausted, fanning myself with some old newspaper as the taxi sped off through the traffic.

The smell of the old car was repugnant, the décor colorful. The fact that there was a Virgin Mary bumper sticker and pictures of what I assumed were the old man's kids and his wife consoled me a little.

He was religious.

He loved his family.

He was probably a hardworking man trying his best to make a living for his family.

People like him didn't do bad stuff.

Then again, I was the idiot who fell for Chase Wright's shit.

My knowledge of the human nature sucked.

I relaxed a little until I noticed the driver's glance in the rearview mirror, catching me looking at his pictures.

"Are you married?" the man asked when he stopped at the traffic lights.

"Um…" I paused, watching the red lights ahead. Should I tell him the truth? I fiddled in my seat, nervously. "I am," I said. "I mean, I only got married like yesterday."

The man's eyes narrowed. He didn't believe me. Of course he wouldn't. What married woman would arrive at an airport—alone?

Obviously, the lying kind.

"Where's your husband?" the driver asked.

"He's waiting for me at the hotel." I forced a smile to my lips, hoping it was convincing enough to fool him. "I work for a paper in the city," I lied. "My boss called me in for some last minute changes. I was barely able to make it out of that office." I waved my hand, like he'd know what I was talking about. "This is my first vacation in seven years. That's how demanding she is."

8

The man gave a short, humorless laugh, completely bored by my made up story.

I couldn't blame him.

I was the worst liar ever.

"You will like it here," he said. "But a young woman like you should always be in companion."

"Yeah, I should be," I muttered and turned my head back to the window, taking in the unknown streets, the unknown territory, a whole lot of unknown everything, some part of me wishing that I had asked Jude to come along with me.

***

Half an hour later, the taxi came to a halt in front of an old, whitewashed building surrounded by a tall wall and an iron wrought gate. I paid the driver and got out, making sure to tip him well in case he was related to some mafia boss who decided I had not paid enough in fares.

I mean, you never knew.

The last thing I needed was another bad surprise. The discovery that Chase was a bad boy who might be after my inheritance was already bad enough. Now I needed some days away from reality, from my old life. I needed time to think how I could possibly divorce him without breaking the stupid contract I'd signed.

9

And for that, I needed to be safe.

His terms had been quite clear: stay married to him for one year and engage in some sexual fantasies of his.

God, I couldn't wait to get divorced.

Does that make me sound crazy?

At least I had negotiated the part about living with him. The way I saw it, I could spend a whole year abroad and never see him.

Pulling the heavy suitcases behind me, I greeted the uniformed security guard, and then I walked up the path to the hotel.

It wasn't the luxury kind.

Far from it.

I would even go as far as saying that it was shabby, which wasn't surprising given that it had been the cheapest hotel I could find.

With my credit cards maxed out I couldn't afford more than a simple room. But it seemed safe and clean—at least I hoped that part was true. It would certainly be more than I could say about the messy life I had left behind in California.

"Hi. My name is Lauren Hanson," I said to the female receptionist and handed her my passport and credit card. "I booked a room last night."

"Welcome to Casa Estevan," the receptionist said in heavily accentuated English. She looked in her forties. Her hair was over-bleached, and her eyebrows looked like they had been tattooed to her forehead. Smiling, she began to type on a computer, and then pushed a few forms and a swipe card over the spotless counter. "This is your room key. Take the stairs to the fifth floor."

The fifth floor?

My eyes swept over my two heavy suitcases.

It would take me half a night to get them up there.

"Could you get someone to take my bags up to my room?" I asked.

She didn't even blink as she grabbed the phone. "Sure. I'm going to call one of the boys to help you." Her phone in hand, she smiled, exposing perfect teeth. "Anything else I can help you with?"

"Er…" I tried not to stare at her eyebrows. Her left one looked way bigger as the right one. It made her look ridiculous. "Can I get some sort of info leaflet?"

"We have none. Sorry."

"Could you maybe give me some pointers so that I can find my way around here?"

She gave a short, annoyed sigh, then put the phone down. "As you wish."

I pushed the card into my handbag as I listened to her recalling the hotel's amenities, making a mental note of the breakfast times and the instructions on how to get to the nearby beach.

"Any more questions?" she asked, her perfectly fake eyebrows slightly raised. As she glanced over my shoulder, I turned to follow her line of vision and noticed that a few guests were waiting for me to finish up.

"I don't think so," I said.

"Have a pleasant stay, then."

"Thank you." I definitely intended to make sure I did. Whispering a "sorry" to the other guests, I made my way to the staircase, unable to shake off the feeling that maybe I should have bought a travel guide or at least spent more money on a room with wireless internet. What kind of person travels to a foreign country without packing at least a tourist guide?

Yeah, me.

Chapter 2

MY ROOM WAS situated on the fifth floor overlooking a dark side street, but if I leaned over the balcony far enough I could almost glimpse a stretch of the blue ocean.

The afternoon sun seeping through the generous windows cast an orange glow on the white bedspread. Opposite from the single bed was a dressing table and a television set. The bed sheets looked plain but clean enough to sleep in. A narrow door led into a tiny walk-in closet.

This was going to be my home for the next days, maybe even weeks.

It was nothing special.

But it was perfect in its simplicity.

Sighing, I collapsed on the bed and crossed my arms behind the back of my head. I knew then that I shouldn't have.

The bed—maybe the intimacy it symbolized or the memory of being with him the night before—instantly drew Chase's face back into my mind, and the mess I was in. I closed my eyes and inhaled a sharp breath, distinctly remembering his lips on mine. They were warm and soft but persistent. His eyes—blue with speckles of gray—reminded me of a dark gray storm hovering over the ocean—wild and untamed.

The knowledge of having been played brought another stab through my chest.

How did that happen?

Because you, Laurie Hanson, have fallen in love with him.

So, his charm had worked on me.

So, I had been stupid enough to believe there could be more between us.

So, he had made me fantasize all the dirty things I wanted him to do to me.

And the final straw—I let him fuck me when I shouldn't have.

But when the vows include all that crap about respect and the guy claims to want to date you, one would think your new, albeit fake, husband would at least have the decency to be honest about his name.

Who was he?

The question had been haunting me since I figured out Chase Wright wasn't who he had claimed to be.

Past internet searches had proven he was an actor, but maybe the sites were fake, too. I had no idea if everything was a sham. I had no idea what to believe any more.

Why did he have so much information about my inheritance?

I had been wondering about that ever since I found the folder.

Should I have given him a chance to explain?

I let out a shaky breath, knowing I wasn't ready. Even the thought of seeing him was unbearable; the risk of believing him even when he might continue to lie too high.

Gullible as I had been, I had to stay away, before my obsession with him morphed into something I didn't want it to be, and I ended up getting even more hurt.

Deep down I had known right from the beginning that I shouldn't trust him. I even knew instinctively that a man as hot as Chase might not be real. However, it should have been a marriage of convenience, a friendship with some great benefits, which is what made me sign up in the first place.

Setting aside the sheer absurdity of its background, I felt used.

Because somehow I'd thought there was—could be— more between us.

I'd thought we had something real going on.

My phone began to ring angrily. Sitting up with my legs pressed against my chest, I leaned back against the bedpost, and peered at my cell phone.

Twenty-three calls, and six text messages.

All from him.

Talk about creepy. Not to mention desperate.

And hot.

Most importantly, hot.

The kind of hot that made my heart race and left me in want.

To talk to him.

To confront him.

To see him—but I wouldn't do any of those. I wasn't a coward, but I wasn't a fool either. I knew that every confrontation, as small as it might be, would be a mistake. Anything related to him would keep me from moving on. As long as I felt something for him, I wasn't ready.

Stupid love.

If only I could renounce it, discard and live without it.

If only I could forget him...the man whose name had been a lie.

Someday, I promised myself, I would meet a man.

Someone with blonde or black hair, brown or green eyes, definitely no broad shoulders, a beer belly—the direct opposite of Chase.

Someone who might not make me forget him in a heartbeat, but who would be worthy of my trust.

My future boyfriend, I decided, would be a strong man with a great character not great looks; someone who would be a philosopher, maybe even with a focus on spiritualism; or maybe some boring guy with a business degree who'd have mostly numbers in his mind rather than chasing the next trophy. Then I'd take a few snapshots of us and post them online—just to show Chase what he'd lost.

But that was my fantasy talking because

a) I doubted Chase was the jealous kind. He told me himself that I was the laurel he liked to chase. He got me so the chase was over.

b) He was a goddamn liar who only cared about himself.

c) See b. All rather self explanatory.

Heck.

I really should call him Loki, I decided. Chase was definitely the God of deceit and lies.

Chapter 3

IT FELT LIKE barely a few minutes had passed since I closed my eyes when a few knocks rapped at the door.

That would be my bags.

"Coming." I jumped to my feet and crossed the room in a few hasty steps.

I threw the door open, ready to motion the bellboy in, but stopped in surprise, frowning.

The man in front of me looked nothing like a porter. He didn't even seem to be local. Dressed in blue jeans and a beige tee shirt that said "Property of Acapulco," he resembled a tourist or a student, judging from the "spring break" logo on his wristband. Judging from his body—lean with broad shoulders—he looked like he was in his early to mid-twenties.

He didn't look bad.

In fact, he was attractive.

Not as hot as Chase, because I was a sucker for gray blue eyes, brown hair, and all the lying bullshit part that came with him, but attractive, nonetheless.

I regarded the guy intently.

His eyes were shielded by black sunglasses, like some cool rock star ready to party all night.

There was something about him that made him look interesting. Unique, I'd say, the way you would look at someone and think "This guy could be the next big thing." Maybe it was his hair. Short, curly, dark brown—he was a less bad ass image of James Franco.

It was the attitude—a bit dreamy, like that of someone who'd spend the night in front of a fire, playing the guitar, enchanting everyone. His stance was relaxed as if nothing could bother him, making you feel you could find your inner goddess just by listening to him.

That an attractive guy like him would knock on my hotel door made me a little wary.

Was he some sort of drug dealer or involved in organized crime?

My heart lurched. For a brief moment, I had the sudden, terrifying vision of him ambushing me, then dumping my body in trash bags, or selling my organs on the black

19

market, then telling his friends, with a beer in his hand, "It was easy as pie. That's why I love tourists who are stupid enough to open the door."

But I could hardly close the door now, could I?

"Yes?" I asked, unsure if he even spoke English.

He pointed to the two suitcases at his feet. "You forgot your bags."

It was only then that I noticed my luggage at his feet.

"Oh." I eyed them as relief streamed through me.

He wasn't some sort of mugger or pimp or worse.

"Where did you find them?" I asked.

"Downstairs where you left them."

"Oh." I narrowed my eyes. "Someone was supposed to bring them up."

"I don't believe they offer this kind of service," he said, his lips twitching with amusement.

It took me a moment to realize he had a sense of humor.

I smiled. "You think the receptionist pulled my leg?"

His expression didn't change as he inclined his head, obviously pondering over possible explanations. "Or maybe she forgot. The lady you spoke to is the owner of this fine establishment. She does all the work here. She does seem a bit over her head at times."

This fine establishment?

He was either being sarcastic or stepped right out of a

20

Jane Austen novel.

"So I gather there's no breakfast either," I remarked more to myself than him.

"There is." He smiled. "But none I would recommend unless you don't mind a bit of diarrhea."

I crossed my arms over my chest, taking him in, interested. His English was flawless, with an undeniably Southern accent. Those damn, sexy sunglasses didn't let me peek behind them to help me read his face. For all I knew, he might be checking out my boobs as he leaned against the wall, cool and composed.

"So, they just left the bags downstairs for anyone to help themselves?" I asked again.

Our topics of conversation were running thin.

He cocked his head to the side. "While it's true that some shady characters might have eyed your luggage, I didn't let them come near it," he said. "I was standing right behind you when you wanted to know when breakfast would be ready."

"Well." I gave a nervous laugh and tucked a stray strand of hair behind my ears, suddenly embarrassed. "I'm starving, and yeah, in general, I'm a hungry person."

"So am I." He let out a laugh, exposing teeth. White, pearly, straight teeth. "Saved me the time to ask her."

"Thanks for doing this," I said, pointing to the bags. "I feel so stupid."

"Don't be. Happened to me before."

"Really?" I said hopeful that he'd elaborate.

He let out a laugh.

A deep, sexy laugh. "Nope," he said and shrugged. "But it's not a big deal. I thought you needed the help and helping you is exactly what I did." He pointed to the bags. "May I? They're heavy."

He didn't wait for my reply. He just picked them up and walked past me, through the open door.

For a second, my fear that he would attack me flickered to life.

He placed the suitcases behind me and returned to his previous position.

"Great," I muttered, unsure what to say.

"Have a great day." He turned and started walking down the corridor.

For a full two seconds I was so stumped I didn't even realize I hadn't thanked him.

"Wait," I shouted after him.

He stopped and turned, his black sunglasses still shielding his eyes. "Yeah?"

"Can I repay you with dinner?" I blurted out, my own boldness shocking myself.

Silence.

What the fuck was I doing?

Of course, he was going to decline. He had to. He knew I didn't

22

mean it.

"You want to repay me by having dinner with me?" Slowly, he walked back to me, regarding me through those unnerving sunglasses.

"Yes," I whispered the word, which sounded more like a question than a statement.

He removed the shades, revealing dark brown eyes that matched his dark hair. He really did look a bit like James Franco.

They could even be related for all I knew. His dark hair fell into his eyes, giving him some kind of haunted look.

I had never been into James Franco, but this guy seemed like someone I might want to spend some time with.

"Yeah. Why not?" He smiled. "There's this tiny restaurant around the corner. See you at seven?"

I took a sharp breath, exhaling slowly. Chase's face popped into my mind.

Liar.

Mr. Fucking. Liar.

If he could lie, why should I stick to his terms? Why should it matter if I had a date or not? Chase might be married to me, but I was still free to do whatever I wanted, to go wherever I longed to, and date whomever I desired.

It was a vacation. My recovery trip.

And to be honest, this guy—he didn't look bad.

And then I realized I didn't even know his name.

"What's your name?" I asked.

"Do you need me to know yours?" he asked.

Did he need to know mine?

What kind of question was that? And then it hit me.

The date wouldn't work out. We would have nothing to talk about because he was as little into this as was I.

Maybe he also needed a rebound.

Maybe he didn't want to get too close to me, just like I wouldn't get too close to him.

"No." I shook my head. "I'm all fine with calling you Bag Man."

"Good, Miss Hungry." He smiled, flipping his shades back, and then he turned, calling over his shoulder, "It's a date, then."

A date.

Crap.

My plane had landed two hours ago, and I already had a date.

I rolled my eyes inwardly, irritated with myself.

Oh, God.

What had I just done? Hanging out with some random guy in some foreign country wasn't exactly the thing ranking high on my to-do list. Not when I had yet to find my way around and I barely spoke more than two words of Spanish.

Why did I have to run away from home?

From myself.

From whatever purpose Chase Wright's lies had served.

But for whatever reason, I also felt excited. Renewed. When Chase deceived me, he took not only my faith. He broke it, and broke it hard. He destroyed every reason, every hope, every desire to be with him. He crushed my soul with one single piece of information.

His lips had consumed me. His touch burned me. His eyes shattered me. Burn and tear and destroy—that was how he broke me in a thousand pieces. Shattered me the only way he knew how—only to rebuild me. To make me someone I didn't recognize. A worse me. A stronger me. A match for his dark side. Only I had no intention to ever be his again.

I would take what he taught me and carve my own path in life. A path that wouldn't cross his.

A path that was all mine.

Chapter 4

THE MOMENT THE door closed I grabbed the phone from the nightstand and dialed the one number I knew I could call day and night.

"You've no idea what I'm going to do today." I sighed into the phone as I let myself fall backward onto the bed, my head sinking into the soft pillow.

"What?" Jude's voice echoed down the line.

"Come on. Have a guess. It's not like there are a million possibilities."

"You got the letters and now you're reading them?"

"No." My laughter died in my throat as my mood plummeted to a new low. "I don't have them yet."

Did she *have* to mention the letters?

Suddenly I wasn't sure I wanted to tell her.

Jude might be my best friend, but did I want her to meddle with my affairs when my life was already turned upside down?

Hell, no.

Knowing her, she'd probably try to sort out my life for me the moment she found out that Chase and I had broken up, in which case all chaos would break loose. But if I kept my personal problems from her, she'd hold it against me forever, and it might cost me our friendship. Did I really want to lose her?

"Laurie, you'd better tell me," Jude said, her tone leaving no room for discussion. "Do you have any idea how worried I am? Chase has been calling me all day with some bullshit about you disappearing on him. He wants to know where you are, and I've no idea what to tell him."

"He wants to know, doesn't he?"

The fucking bastard!

I felt like punching the wall. I had to tread carefully before Chase turned Jude against me like an old, gossipy lady eager to cause trouble and destroy our long friendship. Suddenly, I had the vision of being alone, with nobody to talk to at two a.m. Who was going to be my next two a.m. best friend?

"Yeah," Jude continued. "He had to convince me not to call the cops. Imagine how *that* made me worry, but he wouldn't tell me what happened."

"He's such a concerned friend, our Chase, isn't he?" I said, dryly.

"Wait, are you being sarcastic?"

I grimaced. Nothing ever escaped Jude. "Maybe."

There was a short silence.

When she spoke again, her voice was soft. "What's going on?"

My throat constricted, and unshed tears gathered in my eyes. The knowledge that I had let myself develop feelings for him made me angry. I jumped up from the bed and reached the minibar in a few hasty strides. I didn't care if I owed money for the rest of my life. I needed something. Anything to numb down the anger bubbling below the surface.

My eyes fell on the small bottles of alcohol—just what I needed. I unscrewed a bottle of Tequila and lifted it to my lips. The smell was strong, unpleasant, but it didn't matter.

I wanted to get drunk. Better drunk than a sobbing mess. I took a few gulps of the burning liquid, wincing at the burning aftertaste it left in my throat. My stomach growled in protest, reminding me that I hadn't eaten in a whole day. I eyed the four chips packets, sure that each one would cost me more than my usual weekly shopping.

Then again, for once I didn't care.

I grabbed one, then slumped down on the floor, my

back pressed against the minibar, and tore it open.

"I'm going broke. Real broke, that's what's happening," I mumbled and stuffed a few chips into my mouth, savoring the taste.

"No, what happened between you and Chase?" Jude said.

Hearing his name made me cringe. In fact, every fiber of my body was so tense, I could barely stifle the urge to run for the most secluded place I could find so I'd never have to hear it again. "We…we broke it off," I said.

There was silence on the other end of the line.

"Jude?" I asked, warily. Was she still on? Had she mentally quit our friendship? Because as much as I liked Jude, I had to admit that she had kind of seemed a little too invested in my fake relationship with Chase. At times she had even reminded me of a mother hen watching over her young, or an eighteenth century matriarch trying to marry off her elder duckling of a daughter.

"You did what?" Jude asked carefully, as if she wasn't sure she had heard me right.

The sudden iciness in her voice didn't escape me.

Think matriarch and all.

"Chase and I broke it off," I said with more confidence than I felt. I wasn't afraid of Jude per se; she just had this irritating ability to make me feel bad for things I shouldn't have felt bad about…not least because usually they were none of her business.

"You two did *not* break it off," Jude said slowly.

Which was kind of true, literally speaking.

Not Chase but *I* broke it off, booked a flight, and then I hit the shops right before I boarded a plane, but there was no need to go into specifics.

The thing about specifics is, they always include too much information.

"We're done." I cleared my throat. "You now, over and done with. Finito."

I strained to think of other great words I knew to convey the end of my relationship in the hope that fancy vocabulary would help Jude understand just how much I meant.

"But..." Jude's voice broke off. I rolled my eyes inwardly. She was shocked, which was sort of rendering her monosyllabic. In fact, she sounded aghast. I had never seen her so lost for words. "You were married for less than twenty-four hours."

"Yes." I drew out the word, patiently.

Oh, my god.

She was so right. I couldn't even hold down a fake relationship. I couldn't even commit to caring for a pet. When I'd volunteered as a pet sitter as a means of earning a bit of money during college, the stupid dog ran off. Needless to say, I didn't get the job. Nor the next one.

For some reason, that little embarrassing event reminded me of my love life. Just swap Chase for the dog and me running away instead of him, and voila.

"Things were going so well," Jude wailed. She sounded like she was in mourning.

"Yes." I nodded, even though she couldn't see me.

"And you still have an agreement?"

Uh-huh. Was that the slightest hint of hope in her voice? The denial was back. I couldn't let that happen.

"Yep, but—" I heaved a sigh, considering my words.

Technically, Chase and I still had an agreement, but not the kind she thought we had.

It wasn't a mutual agreement, a wibbly-wobbly, friendshippy kind of thing with a 'nice' guy who was willing to help out a girl in need. What Chase and I had was a contract, a legal binding one with the whole lawyer and court crap hovering over my head, with terms and all that shit. I had been stupid enough to sign the darn thing, agreeing to stay married to the jerk for one full year and have sex with him in exchange for helping me get my mom's letters. The sex he got, meaning I was off the hook. As to the married part?

I groaned.

That one would backfire big time. I couldn't divorce that bad boy for the next twelve months—unless Chase agreed to it, which I doubted, given that he had more hidden intentions and probably more backup plans than the FBI.

My eyes fell on all the energy packed food in the minibar.

Maybe, if I got real fat, real fast, maybe he'd be so concerned about his reputation that he'd divorce me in a heartbeat.

The thought pleased me so much, I pushed a whole handful of chips into my mouth.

I needed to fatten up this goose, and the sooner I started, the better.

Heck, I'd stop shaving my legs, too, and look up on Google habits that would make him beg me to cancel our agreement.

"So let me sum up," Jude said slowly, her mind obviously still processing the big news. "You are married, you have an agreement, and things are going well."

Ah, the bliss of denial.

"Were," I corrected with my mouth full. "They *were* going well, Jude. All in the past. Thou shall not live in the past."

"I don't understand, Laurie," Jude said, taken aback. "If things are going well and you still have an agreement, why would you break it off?"

God, she definitely didn't get the 'past' part.

I shrugged. "It's complicated. Let's just leave it at that."

"So what? All things are complicated, especially relationships. You don't give up on them, just because the road ahead is a bit bumpy. That's the beauty of challenges—you *overcome* them."

I cringed at her choice of words as I pushed another handful of chips into my mouth. "I know, but trust me, this one isn't worth saving. Besides, in all your wisdom you forget that one tiny detail: Chase and I were never in a relationship." I trailed off to let my words sink in, feeling stupid that I even had to explain the situation. "You know this is a fake marriage, right, Jude?"

"Of course I do." Her voice came out all shrill and defensive.

"So, why exactly do you care?" I asked.

And why exactly did I care?

Because you like him more than he likes you. More than you'd ever admit to anyone.

"Why?" Jude asked, jolting me out of my thoughts.

"Why what?" I asked, confused. "Why it's a fake marriage?" I began to massage my temples. We were definitely losing focus here, and that was the last thing I needed. "We hired him, remember?"

"No." Jude drew out the word. "Why did you break it off?"

Oh, for crying out loud.

Why wouldn't she just drop it?

"Because we're not a suitable match." I shrugged again. "Because he's an asshole? Need I go on?"

"No, I know you. You're not telling me everything." Her words rendered me silent. "Something must have happened between you two. Come to think of it, Chase sounded upset. Just like you're upset now."

I snorted.

"I'm not up—" I stopped mid-sentence. Oh wait! Did she just say Chase was upset? "Was he crying or what?"

No idea why, but the thought of Chase crying over me brought on a hysterical fit. I couldn't imagine a stone cold god like him shedding a single tear over any woman, and certainly not over me. Except maybe the kind where he was bent forward, slapping his knees, laughing hysterically over my stupidity.

"I'm serious, Laurie," Jude said annoyed. "I could tell."

"Of course you could." I tossed the empty chips wrapping aside and grabbed another one.

Holy shit, I thought, as I tore it open and peered inside.

There were like five chips in there.

Talk about charging airport prices for half a fried potato. Was that even legal?

But then, was it even legal for Chase to be that hot? Whoever updated the dictionary should also include a section for guys like Chase with the description: hot and dangerous bad boys who liked to melt your panties and toy

34

with your heart only to discard of it the moment they owned it.

"Are you listening?" Jude's voice penetrated my thoughts. I rolled my eyes.

"My dear," I adopted a dramatic, old lady's tone. "Don't trust with your eyes. Look deep into the heart and you will see who he really is. Boys will be boys, but Chase Wright? He's a whole other level kind of trouble." I cleared my throat. "He's an actor, Jude. Remember? I'm sorry, but I'm not buying that Chase is upset. And trust me when I say, neither am I. You know why? Because I don't give a crap about this arrogant bastard or the bullshit he's trying to pull on you."

Or me.

"I don't get it, Laurie," Jude said, baffled. "You were so happy yesterday. You both were. Something changed. I know it did. I could hear it the moment he called me. It sounded like…"

"Like what?" I snapped, annoyed, and tossed the second empty bag of chips aside. My stomach growled, so I grabbed a candy bar from the minibar, then tucked my legs under me to make myself more comfortable.

"Like you finally got rid of your V-card," Jude said slowly.

Was that triumph in her voice?

Shoot me.

Here I was trying to tell her what a jerk Chase had been, and her first thought was that I had sex with him.

My jaw dropped as I stared at the phone speechless.

"Right?" Her tone conveyed hope. "That's what happened? Right, Laurie?" I was so stunned I couldn't reply while Jude continued, "I know first times can suck, because mine sure did, but there's no reason to hide or punish him. It's perfectly normal to feel dirty."

Who said anything about feeling dirty?

Seriously, now she was really making me pissed.

"Punish him? Dirty?" Realizing I was almost shouting, I lowered my voice. "Is that all you were worried about? That I got laid?"

"Isn't that the reason you left?"

"No!"

"No?" she asked, dumbfounded.

"Hell no! You think I'd run away after getting intimate with some guy?" I took a deep breath. "What the fuck?"

"Yes. Laurie, as a matter of fact, I think that's exactly what you'd do."

What? Why would she think that?

"Oh, my god. You just did not say that." I slapped my hand on my forehead and let out a hysterical laugh. "I can't believe you'd think I'd run away just because Chase and I had sex. You make me sound like I couldn't deal with it. With him."

"So, that's not the reason?" Jude asked. Her tone quivered with doubt.

She didn't believe me.

I groaned. "You got it all wrong, as usual. And I'm going to pretend I didn't hear it."

"Oh." She sounded genuinely affected. For a split second, silence ensued.

I relaxed a little. But I should have known better. Jude wasn't someone who'd ever drop a topic—like ever—which made her a big pain in the ass. It was her unrelenting persistence, her unwillingness to give up, that got her far in life and helped her capture the attention of a TV producer. Sometimes, I wished I were like her, minus the annoying, self-centered part. And sometimes I wished I could strangle her just to make her shut up. But more often than not, I was grateful for her intensity and for taking an interest in my life.

It was her way of showing that she cared about me.

"Well, how was it?" Jude's voice drew my attention back to her.

"How was what?"

"Your first time?"

"Seriously? You want to talk about it?" I leaned back and rested my head against the wall. Maybe it had been the alcohol. Or us caught in the moment. Whatever it was that made me do it, that night was the only thing I didn't regret about Chase Wright.

"It was good," I said quietly. "And before you ask the next question, the second time wasn't bad either."

Or the third time that followed shortly after.

"Unfortunately," I added quickly so she wouldn't get the wrong idea.

"I gather he wasn't small or anything?" she asked nonchalantly, as though she didn't care, which couldn't be further from the truth.

Jude always cared about the *tiny* details, or rather the not so tiny ones. She had never made a secret out of the fact that men came with tools she liked to compare and rate.

"What?" I frowned at the empty space. "No, Chase isn't small. I doubt there's anything about him that is small— including his ego."

And ability to lie.

The telltale heat of a blush covered my cheeks as my thoughts trailed back to our one date in his car when I undressed him. That very night I had kneeled in front of him, eager to take him into my mouth and learn all the ways I could please him.

I could still taste him. He had been bigger than I ever imagined, and pulsating with energy—ready to burst, for all the world to see.

Nothing had given me more pleasure than pleasing him—until we fucked.

That had blown my mind completely.

"Why did you break up, Laurie? Just tell me because you're killing me here."

Closing my eyes, I sighed.

That was going to be so difficult.

"Jude," I whispered. "Chase isn't who he says he is."

"What do you mean?" she asked. "No one's ever who they say they are."

"No, this is different." I paused, preparing my words. "He's involved in some real bad ass shit," I said, remembering the call he received. "I don't think he's an actor. All the information we found on Google was fake."

"Of course he's not an actor." She didn't even sound surprised.

My heart gave an almighty thud as the realization dawned on me. I opened my eyes, disbelief flooding through me.

"You knew?" I asked, taken aback.

I could almost hear her nodding. "Yes, I knew. Or how else do you think I made up his ad?"

My heart stopped, then started to race.

I pulled myself up from my lying position.

"What—" I started slowly, my voice breaking. "What ad? Jude, what are you talking about?"

"His online profile," she explained. "I set it up to get you interested enough to hire him. He's not a professional;

just some guy."

I sucked in a sharp breath.

Jude was behind it.

The truth hit me like a train.

Hard.

Fast.

The entire situation felt so surreal, it seemed like a bad dream.

A nightmare from which I'd wake up and realize Jude hadn't betrayed my trust.

"Why would you do that?" I whispered. "And behind my back?" My voice was quivering; my body was shaking. My head was pounding so hard, it felt like a sledgehammer was crushing my skull from the inside.

"Laurie, that was the only way," Jude said.

"The only way for what?" My voice broke again.

"To help you," she explained.

"What the fuck!"

"I'm sorry I did it, but you needed to get married," she explained. "When you just wouldn't shut up about needing a husband, I decided to do something about it. It was my duty as your best friend. If you knew what I was up to, you wouldn't have hired him, but someone needed to get you a fake fiancé to help you out. It needed to be convincing and yes, I thought if he pretended that he was an actor you'd think he was a professional and that it would all work out."

She took a deep, loud breath and let it out slowly. "My point is, I was just trying to help you, so don't be mad."

I shook my head and closed my eyes, feeling like everything I had known in my life was a lie. Here I'd thought I couldn't trust Chase. Turned out I couldn't even trust my own best friend.

"Laurie, are you still there?"

I pulled up my knees and buried my head between them, letting the phone drop to the floor.

My own best friend had set me up with Chase behind my back. I had no idea who was more stupid: Jude or I?

Chapter 5

"LAURIE, SAY SOMETHING. Please don't be mad at me. I tried to help you, I really did," Jude said, sounding emotional when I picked up the phone again.

Was she crying?

Because it sure sounded like it.

"I'm not mad," I whispered, feeling weak. "I'm just trying to figure out why you did it. Do you have any idea what you've done?" My grip around the phone tightened so hard, I feared I might just snap it in two.

"Laurie," she repeated my name as if it was some kind of mantra. "I'm sorry. I really am. I don't know what happened between Chase and you, but I'm sorry for meddling in your affairs. I thought the letters were important to you."

"They are."

It was true. They weren't just important to me. They were all I wanted.

For years, it had been my priority to acquire them. To get them, I had been willing to give up my inheritance just to have something personal from my mother, to read something about her, from her.

"So." I let out a deep breath. "Let's get a few things straight. He's not an actor?"

"No. I created a false profile and linked him to a real actor."

"Well, how did you find him?"

"Through Facebook."

Where all the creeps hung out and you could chat with any one of them at your convenience.

Nice one.

My throat tightened as I felt like another bomb had just been dropped on me and an avalanche was about to bury me alive.

"I was just trying to help you," she repeated. "You would never have approved if you knew what I was up to."

Damn right, I wouldn't have.

I closed my eyes and took a few deep breaths to calm my racing heart.

"On the bright side, you'll get the letters," Jude said. "So it wasn't all for nothing, right? Plus, you got rid of your V-card."

She made it sound like everything was fine.

I shook my head, my fingers tearing at the fringes of the pillow.

"Stop it," I said at last. That instantly shut her up. "You have absolutely no idea what you've done."

Through the awkward silence, I took a long breath as I prepared my next words carefully.

"Chase is Mystery Guy," I whispered. "He's the guy I got stuck in the elevator with."

The silence on the other end of the line barely lasted three seconds. "That's great. At least you found him and the mystery's solved."

"No, nothing's fine, Jude. Please listen to me." My heart crashed against my chest as the image of being trapped in an elevator with no means of escaped flooded my mind. "Chase is the one responsible for the entire floor crashing."

The line stayed silent. A minute passed. Then another.

"You don't know that," she whispered after what felt like an eternity.

"Oh, I'm pretty sure I'm right."

"How?"

"Because I found a folder. It's the reason I left him." I wet my lips nervously. It all happened barely a day ago, so I still felt raw—as if someone had just hurled a bag of rocks at me.

"A folder?" Jude asked. Her voice carried a worried undertone.

"Yes." I paused and cleared my throat to get rid of the shaking in my voice. "It was all in there. My bank account details. Everything about my mother and the estate. The email I received about the interview and the time I would have to be there. I don't think it's a coincidence we got stuck in the elevator. I don't think it's a coincidence at all that the floor crashed."

The line remained silent. I took another breath as the memories came hard and violently—exactly how the last day of my life had been.

"The folder is all the proof I need that Chase was after my money from the start." I pulled my legs up to my chest and wrapped one arm around them, hugging myself. "I didn't give him a chance to explain, but I have proof that he lied to me, and to you, to get me to marry him. To gain my trust. Who knows how far he'd go to get what he wants." The sudden realization sent a shiver through me. I knew nothing about Chase Wright. He could be dangerous. Heck, he probably was. Everything I had held back came crashing down. My hands began to shake. A throbbing sensation settled in my head.

"One hundred people, Jude. That's how many got hurt. I'm so happy… I'm so grateful no one got killed that day, or else I wouldn't know how to live with myself." I wiped a stray tear off my cheek and looked at the moisture on my finger, my mind a million miles away. "He had it all planned. I know he had. If I hadn't found the folder, I would never have discovered that he was behind it."

"Oh, my God," Jude said slowly. "Are you sure?"

Her question sounded more like a statement. She was finally beginning to believe me.

"Yes." I nodded.

"I had no idea." She paused.

"What should I do?" I whispered, more to myself than to her.

"Get divorced. Annul the marriage. I mean, it's only been twenty-four hours." Her tone was gentle. In spite of the monstrosity of the situation, she seemed surprisingly calm.

"No, I can't," I whispered. "Not yet anyway." I felt the question in the air, so I went on to explain the one mistake I had been stupid enough to make. "I signed a contract, so theoretically I'm bound by his terms. It was his condition before getting married. The fool I was, I believed him, so I signed the damn thing." I drew a shaky breath, biding for time before I continued, "So, to answer your question, I can't get divorced for the next twelve months, which of course means that he has access to my inheritance."

"Why didn't you tell me?" Jude whispered.

I shrugged. "I don't know. Why didn't you tell me you found Chase on Facebook?"

"Well, I didn't find Chase per se," Jude explained. "He actually contacted me a while back."

A while back.

What did that mean?

I cocked my head, my interest instantly piqued. "When?"

"Well, I'm not sure when *exactly*, but it's been a while," Jude replied. "But he was already on my friends list when I asked him if he could help you. I don't remember adding him though, but then again I always accept everyone who sends me a friend request, which meant he could have been on my friends list for a long time, way before he even made that comment."

"What comment?"

"Like I said, he was the one who contacted me," Jude said. "I posted a Christmas picture of us two partying. He left a comment to say that we were beautiful. That was half a year ago. I thought it was cute, so I dropped him a message to say thank you. I never thought he'd write back."

I shook my head, unsure if I should laugh or cry. "God, Jude. *Catfish* would have a field day with you. How many fucking Facebook friends do you have?"

She let out a laugh. "Too many. I think I've reached my limit."

"There's a limit?" I asked, surprised. "No, don't answer that one. So he contacted you. What happened next?"

"He replied to ask me if I was your sister, and if you had a boyfriend, because a woman as beautiful as you couldn't possibly be single. And—"

I let out a laugh, interrupting her.

"Oh, my God." I winced in embarrassment, burying my face in my hands. "Please don't tell me you bought that one. I can't believe anyone could be so gullible."

"I'm not gullible." I could almost hear the annoyance in her voice. "Of course I bought it. Why wouldn't I? Anyway, I didn't think much of it. For all I know, he could even be in your friends list."

God, what a creep.

Maybe he had escaped a psychiatric institution. It would explain why he was a stalker.

"Jude, I don't like this," I whispered. "He has all the details of my bank account, and a value estimation of my mother's estate. That means he's some kind of sociopath who plans ahead. I mean, six months? Hello? This guy, whoever he is, is driven by money and he had it all planned out. So don't talk with him anymore."

"But if he wants to know—"

"No, you don't tell him anything. Do you hear me? If he's standing outside the door, you don't open. If he wants to know where I am, you don't tell him. In fact, you block his calls and avoid him. You remove him from your friends list. You block him *everywhere*."

"Okay," she said, and for a moment I imagined her nodding her head as she digested everything I had just told her. "Okay, I can do that. Do you want me to call the cops?"

I let the thought sink in for a moment.

What would happen if she did?

They would listen to Jude's story about Chase, but then what? According to Law and Order and all the crime movies I had ever seen, I knew they wouldn't be able to charge him without some major proof.

Proof—the folder—I was sure would disappear, if it hadn't already. I couldn't believe I just left it behind rather than take it with me.

"No," I said after giving it some thought. "Not yet. Give me time to figure something out."

"All right." She sighed. "Where are you, by the way? I'll finish up early today and can get us some ice cream. We can figure it all out together over a movie."

I sighed as I bit off a chunk of chocolate. The sickeningly sweet taste made me grimace. Our usual nights in. Ice cream and a movie. Under normal circumstances, I would have loved that. "Not today."

Her voice grew wary instantly. "Why? Where are you?"

I tossed the chocolate on the coffee table and took my

time swallowing the chunk in my mouth. "In Acapulco, but that's not why."

She let out a laugh. "You are where?"

"In Mexico." I sighed. "Why are you surprised? It was your idea. And before you ask, yes, I listened to another one of your suggestions. I hope it does me more good than the last time. I'm sorry for not inviting you to come along."

"So you're not coming back today."

"No." I bit on my lip. My throat constricted. I took a sharp breath to calm the sudden tension in my chest. "Jude, I need this break. Clint, Chase, the whole marriage, heck my whole life, it's all become too much. I never had peace. I realized that today. I don't know who I am anymore."

"Of course you know who you are."

"No, I don't," I said, meaning every word of it. "I'm Laurie Hanson, this much I know because it's my name, but I have no home. No place to stay. My parents are dead. I have no family."

"I'm your family, Laurie. You know that."

I hesitated. How could I possibly explain it to her when it took me such a long time to realize it myself? "I know. You're my adopted family. You're also my best friend—the best I could ever have. But you can't help me when I have to find myself. This thing with Chase...I have to make peace with it. Everything in my life was built on struggles and survival. It's not a very stable foundation for the future. I can't continue like this. I have to stop being naïve."

"You're in love with him, aren't you?" Her question came out of nowhere. The air I thought I was holding came out in one big swoosh.

"I...What?" I frowned. "Of course I'm not in love with him." My voice came out too high-pitched, the lie obvious.

"Laurie." Jude's voice was soft. "I'm your friend, not your enemy. You can tell me anything. You know that. I might scold, but I'll never judge."

I turned my face to the window and gazed at the sky for a few moments.

Yes, there had been a time when I thought I could be in love with Chase.

And there had been a time when I thought he could fall in love with me, too.

A tear rolled down my cheek. I wiped it away angrily, but a few more took its place.

I wasn't crying out of pity for myself.

I was crying to cleanse my heart. I was crying to get rid of everything that had been eating away at it.

"I don't love him, Jude. Period. You won't ever hear me say it, so stop asking. Besides, what's the point in talking about it anyway? It's over. We're done."

"He hurt you, and you feel the need to be alone. I get that," she whispered. "But at least let me see you. It's not a good time for you to be alone. I'm going to ask the producers to give me a few days off. We'll take a vacation together."

"No." I shook my head vehemently, even though she couldn't see it. "I really need to be on my own, Jude. I need this break, if only to find myself. To think things through. I don't think I'm strong enough to return to L.A. and face reality just yet. I'm not strong enough to read my mom's letters just yet, or face more struggles."

"You really haven't read them yet?" She sounded unconvinced.

"No. I couldn't," I admitted. "I feel like I need to be in a different frame of mind to read them. It's not the right time. It's not something I can do right now."

"I understand," Jude said.

"You do?"

"Yes. And I'm sorry, Laurie." She paused, as though there was more she wanted to say, but didn't know how. "It's all my fault. If—"

"No. Don't," I cut her off. I couldn't hear another apology, another 'if only.' "I'm as much to blame as you. If I didn't get involved with him and sign the contract, this would never have happened."

"I'm still sorry. I had no idea he was after your money. If I had known, I would never have given him your necklace."

My heart stopped.

I sucked in my breath, my stomach clenching. "You gave him my mom's necklace?"

"I'm sorry, Laurie," she said again. Her voice broke. Was she crying? "He said he wanted to get you a gift and asked me about your favorite kind of jewelry. I said it was your mother's, and that the necklace was broken, and it was his idea to have it repaired, so I gave it to him. I'm going to call him straight away and ask for it."

"No." I shook my head. "Don't contact him. Please."

"But, it's your mom's necklace," she protested.

"I know." My whole chest hurt. I closed my eyes and took a few shaky breaths, feeling as though there wasn't enough oxygen in the room. "I'd rather we stayed away from him."

"I'll get it back without talking. Okay? I promise."

I pressed my lips into a tight line. "I don't want you to do anything, Jude. I don't know who he's involved with, but I don't trust him. Until I have more information, please don't cause me more trouble. Jude, repeat after me: I won't talk with Chase."

"Fine. I won't talk with Chase." I could hear the defiance in her tone. "What's your plan, then?"

"I don't know," I said and shrugged. "Honestly, I'm not sure what to do anymore. I don't know what I want. This thing with Chase…it threw me back in more ways than I could ever have imagined."

53

"You should consult a lawyer."

"I know, and I will, just not now. I couldn't handle it." Least of all talk about him or pour out all the details to a stranger. My mood plummeted at the thought. Time to change the subject. "On the bright side, I have a date today."

"Yeah?" Jude said. "With whom?"

"Some guy who helped me with my bags. He's staying at the same hotel."

"Is he hot?"

"Does it matter?" I tried to recall his face and his dark hair. Was he? I couldn't tell for sure because his image had already become a blur of a memory. "He's kind. Something Chase will never be. This time I'll do it all differently. I want to take it as things come. I'm going out with him and see where that might lead us. I won't make the mistake of hoping for more. I won't expect anything."

"Will you be careful?" she asked, her worry palpable in her tone.

"Of course," I said. "After Chase's betrayal, I doubt any other man could be worse. I doubt *anything* could be worse."

We talked some more, then I finished the call. My own words kept circling in my head for a while longer.

I wished I hadn't said that, because as bad as Chase was, at least I knew where we were standing and how to deal with him.

Chapter 6

BY THE TIME I was done unpacking and had taken a shower, it was already early evening. I locked my few valuable possessions in the safe, squeezed into a black dress, and then gave myself a critical look.

Did I look hot for today's date?

Did it matter?

It was just a date—one of many I was going to have. Chase was a bad boy, so I'd turn into a bad girl. If being a jerk was all that it took to get someone's attention and make them fall in love hard and fast, then it wouldn't be so difficult for me to do the same.

At least that was what I thought as I headed out in search of the restaurant.

I found it just around the corner. What gave away the food's price tag were the cheap "open" neon light in the window, the well-populated bar area in the corner and the music playing in the background. I sat down at one of the empty tables, my back turned to the door. After all, I didn't want to look desperate. You know, the kind of desperate that ended with me in Chase's bed, moaning his name.

At least five minutes passed.

Fifteen.

My date didn't show up.

From my table, I couldn't overlook the entrance area, so I changed to one facing the door, my whole 'not desperate' resolve flying right out the window.

Another fifteen minutes passed. I began to scan the menu, my feet tapping the floor impatiently.

Had he forgotten about our date? Or had he been too much of a coward to decline my invitation? I mean, how hard could it be to say, "Sorry, but I'm not interested."

"Can I get you something?" the waiter asked me again— for the umpteenth time. He didn't look older than twenty.

"Yeah, scotch on the rocks, please."

Sighing, I scanned the menu again, which I was sure I could recite by heart.

The waiter brought me my drink, which I nursed for all of five minutes before dawning it in one gulp.

I had enough—of men, of dates, of anything that

involved romance and sex and everything else that tended to mess with my life.

I ordered the restaurant's 'special' and a glass of red wine. I had just finished my dinner and was halfway through my glass of wine when the door swung open and in walked three guys. The moment the door closed I could feel their gaze on me, scrutinizing the fact that I was in a bar restaurant sitting at a table alone.

"The curse of the single woman," I muttered under my breath and slumped deeper into my seat in the hope I'd magically develop the ability of turning invisible.

"Hola, señorita."

I turned sharply to regard the uniformed guy in his mid-thirties. He was standing so close his naked forearm almost brushed my shoulder. Even in the dim light the gun holster around his waist was clearly visible, drawing my attention to it, and for a moment my heart picked up in speed and my brain struggled to make sense as to what I might have done wrong to catch his attention.

The guy was a cop, so I must have done *something*.

"Sorry, I don't speak Spanish," I said.

"You're lucky I speak English." He plopped down in the seat opposite from mine and waved at his colleagues who were busy ordering drinks at the bar.

"You can have the table. I was about to leave." To prove my point, I slung my handbag over my shoulder and sat up when he leaned over the table, his hand clasping around my wrist.

"Not so fast."

My pulse started to race.

I stared at his fingers as they remained wrapped around my skin.

"Excuse me?" I asked.

"You're such a beautiful girl. Why leave so soon? The night's young." He pointed to my half-finished glass. "And you're not finished."

I frowned at him as I watched his tongue run over his lips.

Oh, for crying out loud.

What was it with me and my tendency to attract all the wrong guys?

First, Chase turned out to be more of a frog than a prince, metaphorically speaking.

Then, my date stood me up.

Now, some cop was trying to chat me up.

And not just any cop.

A Mexican cop who had probably participated in his fair share of dangerous busts and was most certainly used to violence. Or seeing that things went his way.

Something was wrong with the world—or me.

Under normal circumstances I would have told him to get his dirty hands off me but I was in a foreign country and drawing attention to myself was the last thing I wanted.

"You're really pretty," he said and leaned closer until I could feel his breath on my skin. His fingers trailed along my arm. I flinched when he touched my hair to brush it away from my face.

"What do you want?" I asked warily, frozen to the spot as his hand moved from my hair to my shoulder.

"Just a chat?"

He made it sound like a question. Like there'd be way more than a chat later on.

As if.

I swallowed hard and forced a cold smile to my lips. "It's been a long flight. I need to get back to the hotel."

"Where are you staying?" someone asked behind me.

I turned and realized that his two friends had joined him. Unlike the cop, they were wearing jeans, but their hard faces looked threatening enough, as if they would not hesitate to drag someone through the backdoor to beat them to a bloody pulp and then fill out a report about how they acted in 'self-defense.'

"Hey, didn't you hear him? Where are you staying?" the left guy asked, repeating his friend's question.

The alarm bells in my head went off all at once, as my heart started to thump harder. I had nothing to hide. I had done nothing wrong. And yet, here I was, being harassed.

Maybe this restaurant usually attracted only local

clientele.

Maybe those guys didn't like Americans.

Maybe women weren't supposed to sit by themselves.

Heck, maybe it was an offense that I didn't finish my glass of wine.

I shifted uncomfortably in my seat and regarded them for a split second, unsure how to deal with the situation. Finally, I decided I was just going to walk away from a confrontation because, damn it, I had rights.

"None of your business," I said through cringed teeth and tried to get up.

"Answer his question," the cop said. His hand slammed against the table.

I jumped up, scared, and almost knocked over my glass of wine.

Whoa.

Did I detect a hint of a threat in his voice?

And most importantly, what was happening?

"Where are you staying?" the guy asked again.

As if I was so stupid that I'd tell them.

"I'm staying with my fiancé and his parents, "I lied, trying to infuse some confidence into my voice.

"You heard the American," the cop said to his friends as his arm draped over my shoulders. "She's staying with her *fiancé*." I could hear the sarcasm in his voice. "There. Was it so hard to answer the question?"

I swallowed. "Any other questions? Is this some kind of interrogation?"

"Interrogation?" He frowned. "Who said anything about an interrogation? We're just having a little chat."

"If you'll excuse me. I'm very tired." I pulled away from the police guy's grip a little too forcefully. His eyes narrowed on me. After a short glance to his friends, a pulse began to pound visibly in his left temple.

Someone couldn't cope with rejection. Too bad.

"You gentlemen have a lovely evening." I shot them a cold stare and headed out the door, aware of the venomous looks piercing a hole in my back.

Only after I was outside, I dared to exhale the breath I didn't even know I had been holding. This could have ended badly, so I was glad that I was out of there. Shaking my head, I started to walk.

I couldn't wait to get back to the hotel.

Night had fallen and the streets had filled with tourists. Making my way back to the hotel, I pushed my way through the gathered crowds. The moment I walked through the gate I felt a hard grip on my shoulder.

My heart stopped dead in my chest. I turned sharply, a startled cry lodged deep within my throat. But it wasn't some random guy or a mugger.

It was the cop from before.

Alone; his friends nowhere in sight.

"Did you follow me?" I asked the police guy through gritted teeth, barely able to contain my flaring temper.

Who did he think he was, stalking me?

"Show me your bag," he demanded.

"What? No way. It's my bag." I clutched it tighter against my chest, instantly fearing he might be about to rob me, even though that would make no sense. Why would a cop rob me? Unless he thought I had lots of money, which I didn't.

"I said open your bag now." His hand went to his holster, and my eyes widened at his threatening tone.

"Okay." I spread out my palms. "Just relax, dude." My fingers shook as I opened my handbag, exposing its contents for all the world to see. "See. Nothing special. I'm just a tourist. Not even a rich one."

He inched closer to me and grabbed my bag out of my hands. I watched in horror as he began to spill its contents on the street: my calendar, my lipstick, a mirror.

"You don't call this nothing?" He picked up something white.

A card.

On it was a stripper, or maybe not a stripper, but someone who was naked. And a number.

I stared at it, unsure. Where did I get that? I couldn't remember.

"Interesting," he said and flipped it over. Now I saw

what he saw.

It was a card from some sex worker or a pimp.

Even though the text was in Spanish, I was sure that I wasn't wrong.

"Um"—I stared at it, taken aback—"That's not mine."

"Does it matter? All that matters is that it was inside *your* bag." A strange smile played across his lips.

My eyes narrowed as realization dawned on me. "You son of a bitch. *You* put it there."

"I want to see you proving that, my little American friend." His grin widened as he turned me around.

His hands on me sent my pulse racing, and not in a good way. My heart jumped into my throat. I opened my mouth to protest, but the shock coursing through me rendered me speechless.

"You're coming with me." His left hand wandered down my arm to my wrists and he held them in front of me as his right hand fidgeted at his back. "I'll teach you to be reasonable."

"Let go of me," I screeched, struggling in his grip. I didn't realize what he was doing until cold metal snapped around my wrists, the pressure both painful and surprisingly numbing.

I blinked in disbelief as I peered down at the handcuffs. Was he arresting me?

"What the—" My words died in my throat as I was

pulled forward toward the waiting police car and pushed into the backseat.

"You need to come with us on suspicion of soliciting a client and working as a prostitute without a valid work permit," the police guy said and slammed the door behind me.

Fuck!

I had heard of situations like this. People were wrongfully incarcerated. Or kidnapped. Or worse. Why the hell was this happening to me? My breath hitched as my throat constricted with panic.

"I didn't solicit anyone. I'm a US citizen on vacation. Let me out," I screamed and kicked in my seat, ready to draw as much attention to myself as possible. Onlookers had gathered around us, their cell phones suspiciously raised. The videos were probably being uploaded to YouTube that very instant.

My only chance.

I pressed my palms against the window and opened my mouth to explain my situation when the car sped off, siren blaring and all.

Crap.

Double crap.

Remember when I'd said earlier that I doubted any other man could be worse than Chase? Well, I wished I hadn't said that. Turned out that wasn't true at all.

Shit.

Why did I *have* to go for the little black number I was wearing?

Chapter 7

"YOU HAVE ONE phone call," a chubby guy in his late forties said in broken English.

I peeled my aching butt off the cold, concrete floor and marched purposefully for the bars, biting down a snarky remark.

The detention cell had been my residency for all of three hours and already it felt like I had spent most of last month in here. It wasn't just the pungent smell of urine and bacteria that made me want to get the hell out as soon as possible. It was also the fact that not only did no one want to listen to my story of how I couldn't possibly be a hooker; they actually weren't particularly in a hurry to help me prove my innocence.

One phone call.

Make it count, Hanson.

I followed the chubby police officer to a desk and tried not to grimace as my fingers curled around the grubby headpiece of an old phone that had probably seen more unwashed hands than a public toilet door knob.

Who could I call?

I had gone over that decision for hours, mentally scrolling through my limited options, then discarding of each one as I trudged along. Eventually I knew there was only one person who'd run down doors to get me back on US soil.

One person who'd probably get every newspaper and television channel involved to make my story heard and get me the hell out of this hell hole.

Not least because this was all her fault.

She hooked me up with Chase Wright in the first place.

She thought it was a good idea to marry a stranger, albeit a hot one. And then, when I called her from the airport and asked where she'd disappear to if she wanted to hide, she came up with effing Acapulco Beach.

I dialed my friend Jude's number, which I knew by heart and listened to the ringing sound until it went to voicemail.

Apparently she was too busy to answer, or so her voicemail said.

Trust Jude to miss one of the most important phone

calls of my life.

"Hey, Jude. This is Laurie again," I whispered, silently imploring her to pick up. "I know how this sounds, but it's not a prank. I'm still in Mexico, in prison. You need to get me out as soon as possible. Call my lawyer and—"

The line went dead. Confused, I looked from the finger that had just interrupted my call to the smirking police officer.

"Your time's up."

"But I wasn't done. I—" I swallowed hard and clamped my mouth shut in the knowledge that the guy was most certainly not up to date with my criminal status. *I* knew I had done nothing wrong, but he most certainly didn't. And even if he did, I doubted that he cared.

"Fine," I mumbled and followed him back to the detention cell, where I curled up on an uncomfortable chair and pulled my legs to my chest, thinking the chair was less dirty than the stained and sticky tile floor.

Chapter 8

THE DOORS SEEMED to open and close at regular intervals. Women came and went, some cursing, some mumbling, others quiet as zombies. I had tried to talk to the guards several times, then eventually gave up as I realized I wouldn't get more than a glare and a few words I didn't understand.

"Hanson."

Through the fog of tiredness engulfing my brain, it took me a while to grasp that the strange pronunciation was my name. I struggled to my feet and almost toppled forward, inwardly cursing the fact that I hadn't moved from my perched position in what had seemed like hours. With no windows and no working cell phone, I had no idea how much time had passed, but I was thankful for the attention.

Someone was ready to talk to me.

Finally.

"Coming," I croaked, my throat sore and dry.

A hand wrapped around my upper arm and I was guided into the same hall as before. But instead of turning toward the cluster of offices, we walked past those, through barred doors into—

The entrance area.

Holy shit.

My gaze swept around me in a frenzy.

Were they really letting me go, just like that?

"Here's your stuff. You're free to go." A female police officer pushed my handbag into my hand and quickly retreated, her gawk nervous, frightened even.

Jude hadn't come, but she had done it.

A miracle had happened.

Or she had really pulled all the strings.

I couldn't wait to get to the hotel, pack up and leave, because I couldn't get home fast enough to the safety of my boring, jobless and penniless life, and forget all about the little, embarrassing incident I knew I wouldn't tell anyone about.

A smug smile spread across my face. In spite of the stiffness in my bones, I almost danced out the sliding doors into the hot Mexican—

Midday?

I had been in there all night and morning?

I blinked against the glaring brightness as the sun blinded me and bumped into what felt like a statue.

"Whoa, steady there, birdie."

The voice—so deep, so manly—grated on my nerves and made my blood freeze in my veins.

It couldn't be because it was impossible. And yet—

I lifted a hand to shield my eyes from the relentless sun and looked all the way up into gray blue eyes that seemed to shine just as brightly as the sun.

Chase.

Mr. Fucking Liar.

Earth swallow me up whole!

I was so shocked I took a few steps back, then turned.

"What are you doing?" his voice, deep and dark, bellowed behind me.

"I'm going back."

"Fuck, Laurie. No, you won't." His hand clutched my shoulder, stopping me in my tracks.

My hands balled to fists, and for a moment my anger rendered me speechless, though I wasn't sure whether to be angry with myself for calling Jude, with Jude for possibly calling Chase, or with Chase for not realizing that he was the last person on Earth I wanted to see.

"What the hell are you doing here?" I finally managed

through cringed teeth.

"No need to thank me for bailing your ass out of prison." The corners of his mouth curled into an arrogant smirk. I didn't know whether to kiss him or slap that arrogance right out of him.

"Damn right, I won't thank you. In fact, I'd rather go back than see you." I turned my back to him, ready to ascend the stairs and disappear back inside. Countless excuses were already running through my head as how to best to persuade the police officer to let me back in.

Maybe:

"Remember the guy who bailed me out? I have absolutely no idea who that is."

Or:

"I'm too beat to go back to the hotel. Do you mind if I wait inside so I can think hard about all the things I did do wrong because, in all honesty, I still don't know?"

Actually, maybe that wasn't such a good idea. My cell buddy, who I knew for sure was addicted to crack, had managed to smuggle drugs in, and asked me if I wanted to help share them around. She had been quite pushy about it, as if the dirty little packets were no more than herbal tea.

If I were to choose between dealing with her and Chase, which one should I take?

Obviously not Mr. Hot Pants.

I dashed up the stairs and had almost reached the door, when Chase's hand pressed down on my shoulder again. "Whoa, Laurie. You think that's a good idea? They really want to charge you."

I stopped and exhaled a slow breath. "With what?"

"Exposing yourself in a public place, working as a prostitute, trying to solicit a client."

I rolled my eyes. "Obviously, all not true."

"I believe you, but tell that to them." Chase let out a laugh.

Was that the slightest hint of glee I detected?

Oh, my god.

He was laughing at me.

I turned to face him, my face a mask of fury and burning anger. "Who the fuck do you think you are turning up here like this, anyway?"

He didn't even flinch at my icy tone. "I'm your husband, obviously. And as such, it's my duty to make sure you don't spend the next five years in prison for 'soliciting clients', which I know you're not guilty of, otherwise I would have reconsidered my decision." He leaned forward. At first, I thought he was about to kiss me, but instead he whispered in my ear, "What did you do? Smash someone's car to get a cop pissed at you?"

I scowled at him. "I did nothing."

He stood back, eyeing me in puzzlement. "Are you sure

about that? You can be quite hot-headed?"

"I'm so not—" I stopped at his smug expression and shook my head. Maybe I *was* a bit hot-headed. So what? "You don't believe me?" I said instead.

He let out another chortle. "At this point I would believe anything, just not that you were soliciting." He tugged at a stray strand of my hair.

I flinched. "Don't touch me."

"You had something stuck in there," Chase said coolly and held up something pink, then dropped it to our feet. "I believe it was chewing gum. I don't need to impose myself on a woman."

Of course not.

Because no woman in her right mind would decline someone as hot as Chase.

And I was the lucky one to marry him.

Too bad he was a lying bastard.

"Oh." I glared at him. My gaze met his stunning blue gray eyes and my breathing stopped for a few seconds.

Wow.

In the sunlight, his magnetic eyes were even more gorgeous than I remembered.

The last few hours I had tried to make myself believe that it was impossible for someone to be so beautiful. That it was all in my mind because I was so damn attracted to him. That time would open my eyes and help me see him for what he really looked like.

But now?

In real life, he was the most beautiful man I had ever met.

He was also the most wicked—able to transfix people with a mere glance. I wouldn't have been surprised to find out that he had hit on someone to get me out.

"It's great to see you again, Laurie," Chase said nonchalantly, oblivious to my glare.

"How did you convince them to release me?" I asked. "It couldn't have been easy."

He cocked his head, the corner of his lips curling upwards. "I have my resources. And as it happens, I'm also a good actor."

I snorted. "Yeah, more like an amateur. You're not a professional."

"So, Jude told you." He nodded, like Jude's revelation was no big deal.

I smiled coldly. "She told me everything."

"That's impossible. She doesn't know anything about me."

"Like what?" I crossed my arms over my chest and peered into his eyes, challenging him.

"Like that I'm happy to see you again." His gaze brushed the front of my dirty black dress. "How's your vacation been so far?"

I scowled.

He was making fun of me because he knew it'd get to me.

"Why are you here?" I asked, ignoring his attempt at rattling at my self-control.

His brows shot up. "To save you, obviously."

"I didn't need saving."

"It didn't look that way to me," Chase said gently.

I stared at him as I tried to read his caged expression. His words carried a deeper layer to them. I turned around to watch the people walking past, some casting us interested glances.

"All right, you win." I turned back to him and heaved an exasperated sigh. "I'm going back to the hotel, but if you think I'll say thank you, you're wrong. I have no intention of returning home, and particularly not with you. Thank you is about the last thing you'll ever hear from me. I'm going home."

I tried to wriggle my way past him to call a taxi, but he blocked my way—all hard body and stony expression.

"You can't go home just yet."

I narrowed my eyes at him. "Why not? Because you don't want me to?"

"Look—" He took a sharp breath and exhaled it slowly, as he prepared his words. "You'll have to stay for one week in case they want to investigate."

Stay in Acapulco for a week?

After last night's incident, I'd fly home and forget all about it or lock myself in my room out of fear of making another mistake.

"I'm also forced to stay," Chase added quickly. "So, it seems we're both stuck here."

"Poor you."

"I'd say lucky me. I always wanted to see Mexico, and now it looks like we'll have a honeymoon, just like every other married couple."

I scowled at his words.

Married couple.

"Married couple, my ass," I mumbled. "I didn't need saving, Chase. You shouldn't have come."

"I didn't do it for you. I did it for *us*," Chase said slowly, and I rolled my eyes. "I'm your husband. Even if we're only married on paper and you hate me, it doesn't change that little fact."

I gave a snort. "I don't hate you. I don't care for you. That's all."

"I doubt it." He smiled. "When you were in my bed, you liked me…a lot."

I snorted. "That was back *then*. Things have changed in case you haven't noticed. I'm different now."

"No, you're not, Laurie."

I glared at him, hating the fact that he was right. "You

wasted your time coming here. Maybe I did all that and more."

"What?"

"All the things I was accused of," I said.

A dangerous glint appeared in his eyes. "You fucked someone?"

I shrugged. "Maybe. Or maybe I was on a way to a hot date."

"You wouldn't have done that." His mouth tightened. "We have an agreement."

"An agreement which isn't worth shit because you lied about your name." I smiled triumphantly. "For all I know we might not even be married. I mean if Chase isn't your name, then I can annul the contract, right?"

"I dare you to do that and see how far that gets you," he said coldly.

"What's that supposed to mean?"

"That you're wrong."

I raised my chin defiantly. I was wrong pretty often, but I didn't need to hear if from someone as arrogant as Chase. "Wrong about what? That you're a liar and an asshole? I think I have you figured out."

"Wrong about my name," he muttered.

"I'm not wrong. I saw that folder."

"A folder that you shouldn't have read," he remarked angrily.

"A folder that showed you're liar, Chase," I retorted. "I'm so sorry I've ruined all the bad surprises you had in store for me and discovered the motive why you married me."

"Laurie." He placed his hands on my shoulders. I expected his grip to be hard. Instead, it was soft. "You think you know what you're talking about, but trust me, you don't."

I smiled bitterly. "I know enough. All I need to know is that you're a liar." I yanked my shoulders out of his grip. "You might own an entire folder containing stuff that doesn't concern you, but you don't know shit about me, Chase," I said, unable to control the shrill tone of my voice.

Passers-by regarded us, curious, but no one commented. No one stopped to ask an obviously upset female whether everything was okay. I had learned that same lesson last night.

"It doesn't take a folder full of information to know you," Chase said coldly. "You forget I was inside you. Something happened between us. We connected. I felt it and you felt it."

My pulse sped up, but not from the anger that seemed to course through me half of the time I spent in his presence.

In his snug white shirt that accentuated his tan arms and casual jeans, he looked relaxed and comfortable, like this wasn't a situation out of the ordinary and he used to bail people out all the time. He also looked as if he was used to people getting angry with him or maybe he had expected my reaction all along.

The expression in his gray blue eyes seemed lost, though, as if he had no idea what was going on between us.

He looked so innocent, I wanted to scream. This was the man I had married and slept with. The man I had trusted. The man who betrayed me. The man who still tried to manipulate me with sweet words of nothingness.

I could almost still feel him inside my head—inside my body, filling me, taking his pleasure while bringing my own lust to new heights.

The memory of him naked with my legs wrapped around his waist brought the usual tell-late heat to my face. It also brought back the pain of his betrayal, and my promise that I'd never see him again.

"Why are you really here, Chase?" I whispered.

He regarded me for a long moment. "In spite of what you keep thinking, there's no hidden motive."

Only, I knew that wasn't true.

"So you say." I studied his face for a few moments in the knowledge that no matter how many times I asked, he wouldn't tell me. "You know what? Forget it," I said eventually.

Walking past him, I took a left turn and headed into a

back alley, Chase following close behind me.

"Do you even know where you are?" he asked.

I looked around. "Does it matter? I'm going to call a taxi as soon as I see one. So you can stop following me."

"We're not in L.A., Laurie. This can be a dangerous place, as you should know by now. Come on. Let me take you back to the hotel." His fingers curled around my upper arm and pulled me gently to him.

"Don't touch me." I yanked my hand out of his grip.

He stepped back with a hurt expression on his face. For a few seconds we just stared at each other.

Was he faking it?

Was he seriously hurt?

I couldn't tell for sure.

"What did I do wrong?" he asked at last.

"You're asking me? Seriously?" I inched forward, my finger poking his chest.

God, I loved his hard body.

I had almost forgotten how hot he was.

In spite of my anger, I inhaled deeply to catch a whiff of his aftershave. And something else.

His shower gel. Had he taken a shower before coming to pick me up?

And his hair. It looked like he just had a cut.

Why the hell was I even noticing those things?

"I know you lied to me," I whispered. "The least you

82

could have done before you married me is be honest with me and tell me you're Mystery Guy."

"Who?"

"That's the name I gave you after we met in that elevator."

"Nice one." He grinned but I didn't return his smile. His smile died as he caught my expression. "You weren't joking." He grimaced. "Okay, I admit I owe you an explanation for my lies."

The gentleness in his tone touched me, pulled at my heartstrings, but for some reason it also made me angry. A liar admitting or confessing all his lies?

That wasn't going to happen.

Lies are like cobwebs. The moment you take one down, others will take its place. It was impossible for Chase to admit to one lie and be honest when he was cagey about everything else.

"I'm not interested," I said and waved my hand dismissively. "Not anymore. You had your chance to explain everything. You didn't."

"No, you never gave me that chance, Laurie." His tone was accusatory. "You just ran off and left your ring behind." As if to prove his point, his hand slid into his pocket, and he retrieved the ring. My jaw dropped. I stared at the narrow band of gold shimmering in the daylight, imaging him carrying it around with him.

"Why?" I asked.

He frowned, not getting the question.

"Why did you bring it with you?" I clarified.

"Because we're married."

My eyes met his gaze.

And there it was again. That hurt expression that made me feel bad.

God, he really deserved an Oscar for being such a good actor.

Next thing I knew he'd be coming with the whole 'where you end, I begin' kind of crap. No idea whether he ever took acting lessons, but he was definitely talented.

Something broke inside me hard and fast—something I knew would make me forgive Chase. It took all my willpower not to give in.

I glanced at the ring. "You can throw it away. I don't need it anymore."

His eyes narrowed on me again, the hurt expression from before gone—replaced with so much coldness, it was palpable in the air.

His hand closed around the ring.

"Are you sure? Because the way you keep looking at and touching me, it looks like we're still on."

His gaze fell on my hand on his arm.

Holy cow.

When did I touch him?

Damn my body for wanting him the way it did.

Damn Chase for knowing how to evoke the kind of primal instincts I didn't know I even possessed.

I drew my hand back as if I had just been burned, wishing I could do the same with my feelings.

Pull them in, control them, banish them.

"I'm not interested," I said, more resolute. "What I wrote on the paper, I meant it. I want you to stay away from me."

He grimaced, and something flashed across his face.

Disappointment, I realized.

"If you think I'll give you up that easily, you're mistaken," Chase said.

"We'll see about that," I muttered and turned away to the taxi halting at the corner.

Only after taking my seat in the back and slamming the door did I throw a glance back, expecting Chase to be standing here, ready to dash after me. To my surprise, the space was empty.

Like a ghost, he had just disappeared, his last words echoing in my mind.

Chapter 9

I REACHED THE hotel in less than an hour.

The moment I closed the door behind me, I sank on the bed, my arms spread out to either side. As I stared at the ugly stained ceiling, all sorts of thoughts ran through my mind. But it was not the state of the ceiling that kept my attention busy.

It was Chase's words.

Chase's eyes.

Chase's lips.

And his frigging, muscular chest.

How could anyone so physically perfect have such a flawed character? I had never asked him if he worked out, but there was no doubt that he was doing *something* to look so godlike.

Does it even matter, Laurie?

I groaned inwardly. Since meeting Chase, I had asked myself that one question on numerous occasions.

So far from home, I had thought I could escape his allure and get a grip on myself. That I'd stop wanting him. Stop fantasizing about having him inside me, and forget all about his breathtaking eyes, which seemed to undress me at every opportunity.

And yet I found that I couldn't escape the memory of his disappointed expression when I walked away, and the stupid hope that he'd come after me, which he didn't do.

But that wasn't even so bad.

Now that he had bailed me out, new thoughts emerged. Thoughts that were so scary, they confused me, and made me question everything I had found out about him.

Why did he bail me out? He had married me. His mission was already accomplished. Or was there more to it?

I stripped off my clothes and stepped into the shower. The water was hot, relaxing my sore muscles. I don't know how long I stood under a stream of water, my body a shivering mess, my fixation on Chase taking root in my belly, embedding itself deep in my heart.

Chase was like poison.

Seeping into me, infecting me, leaving me with fragments of broken dreams—of hope that there might be more between us.

I was so absorbed in my thought, I didn't hear the door opening.

The shower curtain was drawn aside, and I jumped back, a scream escaping my throat.

I turned and found Chase standing inches from me, watching me with a hungry look in his eyes.

"What the fuck, Chase," I yelled. "You almost gave me a heart attack."

He grinned sheepishly. "I never said I was the quiet kind."

"Quiet? More like creepy." I turned the water faucet off and quickly covered my naked breasts with my hands. "Fucking hell," I muttered to myself. "You're like the devil."

"I've heard he's quite charming, so thank you for the compliment, though I hate to disappoint. I'm quite human." He held out a white towel out of my reach. "Need this?"

I inched forward and grabbed it from him, then wrapped it around my body. My skin was on fire from his intense gaze. I looked up—fury blazing in my eyes.

"What the fuck are you doing here? This is my hotel room. I paid for it. You have no right to break in."

"I didn't break in…" Chase said and leaned against the wall, a smug expression on his face. "Not exactly."

I frowned at his choice of words. "How *did* you get in?"

"With this." His hand moved to his pocket, and he pulled out a key card. It looked exactly like the one I had. "I asked for a visitor card."

"And they gave you one—no questions asked?" I asked incredulously, shaking my head.

"Well, they only had one question, who I was. I told them I'm your husband." His eyes flickered with amusement. "I even offered to provide our marriage certificate as proof, but what can I say? They weren't interested in seeing it."

That was pure madness. I would file a complaint.

Heck, I'd ask for a refund.

"Unbelievable." I shook my head again. "You still have no right to be here."

"Relax, Laurie. I wasn't planning on staying."

"Damn right! You're not." I tightened the towel around my body before it accidentally slipped off, not missing the hooded glance he gave me. A pull settled between my legs. Chase's lips twitched, and his eyebrows rose ever so slightly.

What the fuck was he so smug about?

I followed his line of vision, and to my mortification discovered that my left breast was exposed.

I yanked the towel higher, covering myself up as much as I could, as the heat traveled up my neck and face.

"No need to hide, Laurie. I've already…"

I rolled my eyes, irritated. "Yeah, I know you've already had me."

"I wanted to say, I already told you how sexy you look, but you're right, of course."

The smug bastard.

Of course he wasn't going to miss the opportunity to remind me what had happened between us; what could still be between us if it weren't for me discovering his betrayal.

Knots formed in my stomach.

Suddenly, the bathroom felt too cramped.

I needed to get out.

Pressing the towel against my body, I stepped out of the shower cabin, making sure not to get too close to him, and started to wring my dripping wet hair in front of my mirror, my gaze avoiding him.

"Well, I hope you got a good look, because you won't get to touch me again," I muttered.

My gaze brushed his in the mirror.

I had expected to see disappointment, maybe even anger, instead a flicker of amusement flickered in his eyes.

"Are you sure about that?" A smile tugged at the corner of his lips. "As far as I remember, you were the one asking me to touch you. Maybe not so much to touch as to fuck you. I believe your exact words were 'I want you to be my first'."

As I stared at his reflection in the mirror my cheeks

flamed. "For your information, I just wanted to get it over and done with. It had nothing to do with you. It could as well have happened with anyone. No offense, Chase, but you were just a means to an end."

"None taken." He inclined his head in mock-thought. "I won't deny it that I'm glad it was me because I doubt you would have had so much fun with someone else."

"How would you know that?" I turned to regard him, my lips pursed. "Maybe I faked it."

"Considering my experience and the little sounds you made, I doubt anything about our session was fake."

I stared at him, my words failing me. Forget the experience part. "I made sounds?"

His lips twitched. "No worries, they were cute." He lifted a hand, as though to touch me, then dropped it again, his tone mocking. "My only advice for you, next time scream a little louder. It can be a real turn on."

"You're…" My expletives remained trapped in my throat. "There won't be a next time."

"So you say." His eyes glinted with a hint of challenge. "Maybe I should say challenge accepted?"

I scowled, heat creeping into my bones. "It happened once. It won't happen again. And when I say that, I mean as in 'never'." I squeezed past him and dashed to the bedroom to get dressed.

"Why not?" he asked, following close behind me.

"Because I'm no longer interested in you."

"If you're so impartial, why don't you remove that towel? I want to see your lack of excitement at the thought of my tongue licking you all over," Chase said.

The image entered my mind too easily.

Oh, God.

That was the last thing I'd ever do.

Struggling to fight my labored breathing, I walked into the tiny walk-in closet and switched on the lights.

"Surely if you feel nothing, want nothing, it shouldn't matter whether I see you naked or not," Chase persevered.

I turned around, forcing my brain to come up with some witty response, but he was faster and beat me to it.

"Thought so, Laurie."

I peered into his gorgeous eyes. They were mocking but gentle, his expression soft.

Everything in that room stopped still, and it was as if time did, too. It was in that moment I realized how much I still loved him.

As if sensing my emotional undercurrents, Chase moved closer and brushed a wet strand of hair out of my face.

"I know you still want me, Laurie," he said tenderly. "I won't make a secret that you're still on my mind, too."

My breath hitched, whether it was from the lack of space or from the intimacy, I couldn't tell.

"You're delusional," I managed to croak, which was

rewarded with a chuckle.

"No, my mind's perfectly clear on what I want and what you need."

Oh, the arrogance.

I had to change the topic—and fast—before his lips, so awfully close, would crash upon mine. That was something I imagined would happen. If he kept doing what he did, his hands playing with my hair, his eyes on my lips, speaking the kind of words I wanted to hear, I'd lose all self-control and kiss him, because the truth was…he was right.

My knees were weak. My heart was racing. Deep inside I could feel hundreds of butterflies fluttering, pounding against the fragile shield I had learned to build in the past.

"What do you want, Chase?"

He hesitated. Dropping his hand, he took a step back and leaned against the wall, his posture implying that he had no intention of leaving anytime soon.

"Why do you assume I want something?" Chase asked.

I stared at him. "Are you serious? You had a folder with an estimate of what my inheritance is worth."

His lips tightened, and a guilty expression fell on his face. At last he crossed his arms over his chest, his eyes avoiding me.

I used the silence to search for the most oversized piece of clothing I had, and found nothing in the mess I had left behind the night before.

A thong fell from between my clothes. Chase picked it up and lifted it to inspect it. I thought I might just die from mortification.

"Are you kidding me? Give it back." I yanked it out of his hands.

Unfazed, he sifted through my clothes until he found a short, red dress that belonged to Jude. "You should wear it today."

I grabbed it from him, meeting his gaze. "Stop touching my things, okay? I'm not going out with you."

"It was merely a suggestion." His eyes sparkled with delight. I braced myself for another one of his suggestions, but none came. Instead, his gaze remained glued to my every move. Up close, he smelled fantastic—a deep, manly scent.

A deep pull settled between my legs.

I wanted him so bad, it hurt, and yet I couldn't act on my desire.

I really had to change the topic—do whatever it took to distract myself from my stupid attraction to him.

"You didn't answer my first question. What are you doing here?" I found a pair of jeans and a top

"Relax, Laurie. I have no intention of staying here."

I squeezed my clothes against my chest, the layers of fabric helping to strengthen my mental barrier. "You still had no right to come and see me."

"You're right." Something hard flashed across his face. He tried to hide it by turning his back to me and walking out of the closet, but I caught it nonetheless. I thought he had left so I peered out. He regarded me from the minibar, which I had raided earlier.

"May I?" He pointed to a bottle of something.

"I'm going to change." I shrugged, not bothering to answer.

While he kept himself busy with the bottles and glasses, I used the opportunity to dress quickly, all the while listening to make sure he wouldn't try to come in.

But my fear was unfounded.

He left me alone.

He didn't look.

Not once.

He gave me all the privacy I needed.

When I returned to the bedroom, he was sitting on the bed, two glasses of alcohol in his hand, his gaze focused on the floor. He passed me my glass, then patted the space next to him. "Sit down."

Under different circumstances I wouldn't have followed his command, but there was something in his voice—an urgency—that made me listen to him.

That, and the fact that the room had no other sitting opportunities.

It was just the bed—a bitter reminder of our time

together.

At last, I sat down, watching him. In the silence of the room, he took a few sips from his glass, his gaze avoiding me.

"I admit I wasn't always truthful," he started. "I admit a few wrong things."

"You married me to get my inheritance," I said coldly.

"I can't deny that," he whispered and closed his eyes. "But it needed to be done."

Tears began to sting my eyes, and bitterness rose in my chest. Somewhere at the brink of my mind, I realized that everything I had feared was true. He had been after my inheritance all along. He had used me. And now he was talking more bullshit.

"Wow. You're an asshole." I almost choked on my voice. "You don't even try to claim otherwise."

"I told you a few lies, Laurie. But not everything I told you was a lie." He took a deep breath. I could see that he was struggling with something.

"Yeah?" My eyebrows shot up, my voice dripping with bitterness. "Like what?"

"Like the fact that I'd never harm you."

"Really?" I laughed. "Liar."

He lifted the glass to his lips, but didn't take a sip. "It's not a lie." He frowned. "I really like you."

"Liar."

He turned his head to me, his eyes meeting mine. "Not a liar enough to know that I'm attracted to you. I'm also not afraid to show it, as opposed to you."

"Liar," I whispered again. "And I'm not attracted to you, which is why there's nothing to show."

His eyes narrowed on me. "Now, who's the liar here? I know for a fact you're attracted to me."

His ego was taking new proportions.

"How would you even know that?" That he thought so made me angry.

"I can feel it." His fingers brushed my neck. His touch, warm against my still damp skin, felt electrifying. "The moment I met you, I knew something would happen between us. Trust me, I didn't mean for this to happen. I was never supposed to fall for you, Laurie."

His words caught me off guard, and my heart gave another almighty thud.

He was playing with me. He had to be because Chase Wright couldn't possibly have feelings for me.

And yet, for a moment, I wished I could believe him.

"I can't say I'm sorry for what I did," he whispered. "I can't even say I'm sorry for being attracted to you or for fucking you. I know you have many questions, and I'll be more than happy to explain."

I closed my eyes. My head was spinning with the same thought.

He had married me for my inheritance.

"I can't," I whispered.

"I'm still the same man, Laurie."

I let out a sarcastic laugh. "No, you're not. You're someone I don't know."

"Meet me in an hour, and I'll show you who I really am. I'll explain everything."

"Even if I let you explain, you really think I'd believe you?"

"Yes," he said quietly. "You trusted me with your virginity, and now I ask that you trust me once more."

"You compare my virginity to your deception?" I laughed. "Nice try."

"Please, Laurie." He looked at me. "We still have a contract. I know you have feelings for me."

I rolled my eyes. "You should really have been an actor, Chase, or should I call you Kade?"

He gave an exasperated sigh and stood. "I already told you my name's Chase."

"No, it isn't."

He cocked his head, his tone low and dangerous. "How would you know?"

"Because I do. I'd rather trust my instincts than you."

"Well, you have your information wrong," Chase said coolly.

My mouth clamped shut. I eyed him cagily, my thoughts

racing.

If Chase was his real name, then that could mean that things might still be the same between us. He was still my husband. We were legally married.

"Look, Laurie. I owe you an explanation," Chase said, interrupting my disturbing trail of thoughts. "It's one of the reasons I came here to see you."

I shook my head as I remembered my resolve. "I'm not interested in your reasons. What matters to me is that you lied to get close to me. That was all I needed to know."

He frowned and something flashed across his handsome face. "Aren't you the slightest bit interested?"

"I am. In fact, I'm very curious," I said. There was no point in denying the obvious. "I'm just not interested in hearing more of your lies. Seeing that you lied once, how can I possibly trust your words again?"

"You have no guarantees. You'll just have to believe me."

Nodding, I smiled grimly. "That's true, but I'm not willing to do that. So stop asking me to meet with you. Because I won't." My voice broke and I cleared my throat to get rid of the lump lodged inside. "I won't get involved with you again."

"I don't believe you."

I laughed, the bitterness creeping into my tone even though I didn't want him to see just how affected I was.

Somewhere at the back of my mind, countless alarm bells went off, and bitterness settled in my chest.

I got up, my thoughts racing, my heart breaking as I spoke the words I had prepared.

"It was just sex, Chase," I whispered. "We fucked. We had a good time. And then I left. People do it all the time. Get over it. Maybe last night I was ready to repeat the experience with someone else, and the guy just wasn't that into me." I shrugged as I stared him down.

His blue eyes turned into icicles. If looks could kill, he'd have me pinned to the ground fighting for my life.

"I know you. You might be a lot of things, but you're not *that*." His voice came low, definite. I had never seen him so angry. Then again, his anger was no match for mine.

What the fuck was 'a lot of things' supposed to mean? And why not 'that?'

How could I fight against his overconfidence when it became a lost battle the moment I let him be my first?

How could I fight with myself when my feelings pushed me to do things my mind didn't want to?

"You don't know me at all, Chase," I reminded him.

"I believe I know you better than anyone else," he said coldly. "Correct me if I'm wrong, but when we were stuck in that elevator, you told me secrets you've never told anyone else."

My jaw dropped, and then closed again.

My whole being was on fire, twisting, shaking, as I watched him stand.

"Get dressed, Laurie. I'll pick you up for lunch in an hour."

An order. Cool. Composed.

Fuck it. He was hot as hell.

I stared at him. "Why do you think I'd ever do what you say?"

"Because you want to get rid of me." That rendered me silent. "I'll only leave after telling you why I did what I did. Beside bailing your pretty little ass out of jail, it's the least I can do for you."

"I didn't need your pity. I'd have—"

"Stop being difficult," he cut me off and wrapped his arms around me, pressing me against him, so close I could barely breathe. "I owe you an explanation, okay? So you'll get one. And then, only then, I'm going to leave because that's what you want. Deal?"

I drew a sharp breath, ready for another snarky reply, but no words came out.

His words had affected me in more ways than I cared to admit.

No, scratch that.

His presence pulled at all my strings. Everything about him did. His gaze. His breath on my skin. The way his eyes seemed to brush over my lips, leaving them tingly and in dire want of his kiss.

Cradled in his arms, with my head leaned back to glance all the way up into his eyes, I could feel the heat eradicating from his body. I could feel the layers of my anger melting and my resolve slowly fading.

His gentle touch on my arm was a direct opposite to the cold stare he gave me.

"So, I gather I have no choice?" I asked.

"No."

I sighed, my chest strangely heavy, my voice choked. "Just answer me this: Who are you? Is Chase really your real name?"

Hesitating, he let go of me, his blue eyes shimmering like an ocean in the morning sun focused on me. He was fighting with himself, probably wondering whether to disclose the truth or how much to tell me.

"Not here, Laurie," he whispered. "I'll pick you up at twelve. And wear the red dress." The tone of his voice was strangely soothing and built an unnerving contradiction to the grip he still had on my upper arm. And then he let go of me and walked out, closing the door behind him.

As if I was the one intruding on him.

For a long time, I stood frozen to the spot, my mind processing.

The truth was, I wanted to know. I wanted more. And yes, my pride and ego were standing in my way, as well as my fear that giving in could mean I might lose myself again—that I might get lost in Chase's eyes, in his being, in everything he had to offer.

I felt a strong need to call Jude even though she wouldn't know what to tell me because no one could possibly understand just how torn I was. She sure wasn't the one fighting the arrays of emotions inside me; she didn't have to cope with the fear of being lied to again in the future, or face the risk of believing him in the knowledge that truth isn't easily distinguished from a lie.

And most importantly, the fear of the known.

Once he explained his motives, would I be strong enough to walk away?

Did I even want to leave him behind?

Somehow I sensed that I would have to very soon, but whether I wanted to, whether I was strong enough to, whether I could do it—that was a different matter.

Chapter 10

THE MOMENT CHASE was gone, I called Jude with the update.

"I'm so stupid." I groaned into the phone. "I'm going to see him again."

I still couldn't believe it.

Less than thirty-six hours ago, I'd watched the world through pink-colored glasses in the hope for a great future. Now that they had been ripped off my eyes, I was still pining for Chase.

Mystery guy.

Bad boy.

Mr. fucking liar.

Those were all the names that came to my mind when

thinking of him.

Those and Mr. Tall, Handsome and Mysterious, even though, if we were absolutely honest, his tongue deserved a mention, too. The way it could bring me straight to pleasure heaven, it had been nothing short of a miracle.

Fuck.

Just thinking about it made me wet.

It was a god's gift—and not the good kind—sent into the world to torture and remind me that I was a weak, gullible woman. And not a woman with a soft spot for bad boys, but a woman with raging hormones and all that wasn't holy. Yes, it was most certainly my frigging hormones that had made me so wildly in lust for Chase that I switched off all rational thoughts and just let him fuck me.

"I should call him and tell him our meeting is off," I continued to rant. "After all he's done, it looks like I'm still dating him, or maybe not dating—" I tapped a finger against my lips in thought. "Anyway, seeing him is the last thing I should do. I swear it's a mistake."

"No doubt about it," Jude agreed on the other end of the line. "But maybe just listen to him. You know, get his side of the story. Maybe it isn't as bad as you think it is. Maybe you're making a big deal out of nothing. Who knows? For all we know, he wanted to marry you because he's a collector, and you had an old painting in your family heritage that he desperately needed to acquire."

"Which would be exactly the same thing as marrying me for my money." I gave a short, loud snort. "If that had been the case, he'd only have had to ask me, and I would have gladly given it to him because you know how much I hate old stuff." I looked at the watch again.

Five more minutes.

I could feel the onset of a panic.

"Just give him a chance," Jude insisted. "Promise me, Laurie. The last thing I want you to feel is regret. Nothing good ever comes out of it. Trust me on that. I know you said you don't have feelings for him, but honestly, I don't believe you."

"Is that why you called him to bail me out? And don't tell me you didn't, because I know you were behind it."

"I…" She sighed. "I felt bad for going behind your back. Plus, it was your mom's necklace and it was all my fault and—"

"Keep it short, Jude," I said impatiently.

"Fine," she replied. "I called him."

"Oh, Jude," I exclaimed. "Why can't you ever listen to me and stay out of my crappy life?"

"I know. I know. And of course you're right," she said, her tone slightly irritated. "But in my defense I'll have to stress that it was already out of my hands."

"How so?" I asked.

"When I called him, he already knew you were in jail,

106

and he was on his drive to the airport."

"Really?"

"Yep."

"How would he know that?" I asked, agog.

"That's what I wanted to know, too," she said thoughtfully. "He said they called him because he was listed as your husband. Even if I wanted to, he was the only person allowed to bail you out. Their words. Not mine. I even called to check up the fact. So, even if I wanted to, I would not have been able to help you."

That sounded like utter bullshit.

I blinked several times.

"Now I really do owe him, don't I?" I said flatly, feeling weak at the thought of having to repay Chase. It was the last thing I needed when all I wanted was a clean breakup.

"No," Jude added quickly. "Definitely not. I'd say he still owes you for the crap he pulled on you."

"You really mean that?" I asked.

"Of course, I'm your friend, aren't I?"

Which was why her reasoning was biased and couldn't be applied in real life.

"Thank you." I smiled. "That was exactly what I needed to hear." I glanced at my watch again.

I only had four minutes left.

"I've got to go," I said. "I'll call you as soon as I'm back. Wish me luck."

"Laurie?"

"Yeah?"

The line remained silent for a few moments as I waited for the kind of words I knew would try to change my mind about him.

"I don't expect you to forgive him," Jude said softly. "Just hear his side of the story, okay? And don't run off again and end up God knows where. You scared the hell out of me. Don't do that ever again. Yes, it was my idea, but I didn't think you'd go for it."

I let out a laugh and got off the phone, then leaned back.

Was this a mistake?

No doubt about it. But the truth was, Jude was right.

Chase harbored more secrets than the ancient Druids.

I didn't want to be wrong and judge him without hearing his side of the story. And then, there was my curiosity, my annoying and desperate desire to know what was going on.

Was it possibly some harmless misunderstanding?

Were his parents pushing him for a marriage for a reason unknown to me and he had no other choice than to wed a stranger?

Even if Chase wouldn't explain everything, at least there was the slight chance that I'd get a few morsels of information. Then I'd do what was necessary—research, take apart the pieces of information I had, and decide what to do with them. Leave and forget. Or work with them, and create something better.

Slipping into a light blue halter neck dress, definitely not the red one Chase required, I checked my reflection in the mirror. My hair, which was usually twisted into a practical, loose side bun, cascaded down my shoulders. Even though I barely had seen the sun, my skin had a light bronze glow to it. My cheeks were flushed. If one didn't dig too deep, but judged from my fake smile, I could have easily passed as the happy, recently married bride.

Bride.

The word stung.

I was a bride, just not a traditional one. Not even a happy one. Even with all the fluttering in my stomach at the prospect of soon seeing Chase, the situation was what it was.

"Stupid," I muttered and applied another layer of lip gloss, then stood back to inspect the result.

What was I doing? Making an effort for a fake husband?

"Just stupid." I wiped my thumb over my red lips in an effort to wipe off the color.

A rap at the door.

My head snapped toward the hallway.

Someone was banging at my door. I glanced at the watch.

Chase was here, though a minute late.

"Coming," I called out and retrieved my handbag from a nearby chair.

I reached the door in a few, hasty strides. My heart was racing but not from the effort. My stomach twisted slightly at the thought of spending more time with him.

Truth be told, I was more looking forward to it than I should have been.

Taking a deep breath to settle my nerves, I swept my hair sideways and grabbed the doorknob. When I opened the door, my breath caught in my throat.

Standing in front of me wasn't Chase. It was the guy I had asked out on a date the night before. Dressed in a suit, he looked like he was headed to an important meeting. He looked serious, completely different. The change threw me off. It was safe to say I wouldn't have recognized him if it weren't for the stupid black sunglasses he was wearing.

"Oh…Hi?" I cocked my head in surprise, unsure what else to say.

What do you say to someone who didn't turn up to a date?

He nodded approvingly as he checked me out, or at least that's what I believe he was doing.

"You look nice." He pushed the glasses to the top of his head, and his warm brown eyes met mine.

"Thank you?" I shifted uncomfortably, my hands

fiddling with the doorknob. "Did we arrange something for today?"

"No, that's why I'm here." He smiled. "I wanted to apologize for standing you up."

"It's not a big deal." I shrugged as if it didn't matter. "I understand you forgot, or whatever."

He shook his head, his eyes penetrating. "No, I didn't forget. An emergency came up."

An emergency during his vacation?

Seriously?

That was the crappiest excuse I had ever heard.

What the hell was wrong with my stars? Why did they keep sending me guys who found it so easy to lie to me, stood me up or deceived me? And most importantly, what the hell had I been thinking going out on a date with some random guy whose name I didn't know?

"It's fine." I said, forcing another smile to my lips. "It can happen to anyone."

"I would have called you if I had your number," he continued.

He even looked sincere as he said it.

"Honestly, it's fine," I repeated. "I had plans anyway."

Yeah, getting locked up.

"I want to repay you with dinner. What about tonight?" His smile morphed into a grin. "Or now. Special treat. Best place in town?"

"Um…" My hand tightened on the doorknob. Obviously, I couldn't meet him now, even if I wanted to. Not when Chase could be here any minute, and my trip so far had been anything but fun. I wet my lips nervously, deciding to stick to the truth.

"Now isn't a good time. Maybe another day."

He got the hint.

I could tell from the way his eyes narrowed ever so slightly, but his smile didn't vanish.

"You know what? Let me give you my number and you can call me anytime if you have a change of heart."

"Um, sure." I held up my phone and swiped my thumb over the screen to unlock it.

"What the fuck!" a male voice boomed behind us. My hand froze. In fact, my whole body did. I turned my head and saw Chase striding toward us, his face a mask of fury. Come to think of it, he looked like a raging bull. I frowned.

Whoa!

Was he jealous? It couldn't be, and yet, the moment he reached me, his hand went possessively around my waist, almost cutting off my air supply.

"What are you doing here?" His voice was so cold every vein in my body froze.

I frowned at him. "It's none of your business. I can do whatever I want."

"I'm not talking with you," he mumbled at me as he

turned to the other guy. "What are *you* doing here?"

I stared at Chase, then at the guy who had stood me up, my glance going back and forth between them. My heartbeat sped up as a sense of dread nestled in my stomach.

Judging from their tense postures and how close they were standing to each other, I sensed they knew each other. The other guy's lips tightened, and his hands balled to fists, and for a second, I feared a fight would erupt.

"What's going on?" I asked warily, even though I couldn't decide whether it was really a good idea to get involved and break the icy silence between them.

No one bothered to reply.

It was as if I didn't exist.

At last, the guy lifted both his hands in mock surrender. "She's all yours." He flipped his glasses back on the bridge of his nose. "Have fun." And then he started to walk backwards, arms wide. As he reached the corner, he turned and disappeared from our line of vision.

I looked at Chase questioningly, but his expression was stony and icy, his body tense. Somewhere, a door slammed. The guy had probably returned to his room.

I turned to Chase, eyeing him inquiringly. A pulse throbbed underneath his eyes, and a muscle worked in his jaw.

"What was that?" I asked.

113

"Nothing," Chase said through gritted teeth.

"I don't think that was nothing. He brought my bags to my room the day I arrived, and we had a little chat."

"Nice. Good for you." He turned to me, his tone sarcastic and cold. "Did you go out with him?"

He sounded so pissed, I flinched.

Opening my mouth, I frowned, but my reply came too late. Chase's gaze hardened, if that was even possible. "No, don't."

"Are you sure that was nothing?" I asked.

"Yeah," he whispered.

I could feel the waves of anger wafting from him.

"Chase." I let out a deep breath. "You don't own me. You know that, right?"

"Right." He was being uncharacteristically monosyllabic as he forced a fake smile on his lips. "What was I thinking? You should have told me you were going out with my brother."

My jaw dropped, and my knees went weak. I felt as though someone had just pulled a rug from under me.

"*That* was your brother?" I asked in disbelief.

He nodded and raked a hand through his hair.

His beautiful, short brown that I loved so much.

"But…you…you don't look alike," I stammered.

"Yeah. We get that often." His eyes narrowed on me and something hard flashed across his face. "*Why* are you

114

asking? Do you want Kade's number?"

I stared at Chase, unable to digest what had just happened. My body felt numb, as though I had just been pushed into ice cold water. A cold, slick layer of sweat covered my body, making me tremble.

"Wait…" I took a deep breath to calm the sinking sensation in my stomach. "*That* was Kade? Kade is your brother?"

"Yeah." He smiled grimly and grabbed my hand again. "The one and only."

Crap.

My stars really sucked.

Chapter 11

"CHASE. STOP." I yanked my hand out of his, forcing him to stop at the staircase. My head spun, my throat closed in, and my breath came in short, shallow gasps. My body tensed as my fingers touched his back. His shoulders were rigid, but he turned to face me, his expression gloomy.

I planted my feet into the floor to steady myself for another confrontation with him, and dropped my hand.

I couldn't believe it.

Basically, the guy I had tried to get a date with was my brother-in-law.

Really, under what kind of frigging stars had I been born?

"Kade." Feeling faint, I almost choked on that word as I

searched Chase's angry face for a sign that it was all a misunderstanding. "That was the name on the note."

His eyes narrowed and something flashed across his face again. Slowly, he closed his eyes and muttered something that sounded like 'fuck,' but I couldn't tell for sure. His reaction confirmed my fears. He was still willing to lie to me. He harbored no intention of opening up to me any time soon.

I had no time for his bullshit. I had no more patience for hot guys and their mind games.

Husband or not, Chase Wright was the past. He had to go.

"Fuck you," I muttered and turned around.

His fingers clasped around my upper arm, the iron grip sending an unpleasant sensation through my arm, like my blood supply had been cut off.

"I know how it looks, Laurie," he said.

I turned back to regard him, my gaze filled with daggers of ice.

"Do you?" My voice started to rise as I pulled my arm out of his grip. "I think you have no idea, in which case let me paint the picture for you. You had me followed all the way from home."

"No, Laurie. No." He shook his head vehemently and pressed his palm against his chest, right where his heart was located. "I had no idea he was here." He caught my

117

doubtful look. "Or that Kaiden had you followed."

I crossed my arms over my chest, shaking my head. "Kaiden? I thought his name was Kade."

"Kade is Kaiden's nickname." He blinked at my cold expression. "What?"

"Why should I believe you?"

"Because it's the truth," he said. "Trust me when I say I had absolutely no idea he was here."

I laughed. I was ready to trust him all right. "He's your accomplice."

"Accomplice?" His eyebrows rose ever so slightly at the word. "That's a big word for my brother, particularly since he always had my back."

"I don't think there's one more suitable, considering he's probably the guy who called you. Did he send you the pics that had our faces circled with a red marker or will you pretend you don't know who did that, either?"

"The pics?" Confusion crossed his features. "You know they were from your stepfather, right?" His eyes narrowed. "And what phone call are we talking about?"

I swallowed hard as I realized that I had just blurted out the truth.

"Did you go through my phone, Laurie?" Chase asked slowly.

For a moment, I just stared at him. Of course, I could just deny it, but what was the point? The things he had

118

done were so much worse.

"Not on purpose," I said. "It rang, and I assumed it was my phone so I picked up."

I eyed him carefully, not sure why I felt guilty when it was the truth. Besides, I had every reason to be angry *at* him, not the other way round. There was no way I'd feel bad at stumbling over something that had helped me realize the whole *fake* marriage was a *sham*.

Talk about irony.

Oh wait…

"Are you trying to change the subject right now?" I asked. "Because I can tell you it's not working. I—"

He pressed a finger to my lips, cutting me off. "I believe you." He cocked his head, his lips twitching. "See how easy it is? That's how I want our relationship to be—trusting and forgiving, with a sprinkle of hope."

Sprinkle of hope.

Who talked like that?

"Let me guess, you want the whole 'agree to disagree' crap, too?" I asked, my voice oozing sarcasm.

He smiled. "Wow, you're reading my mind now."

I stared at him, unsure if it would get me into prison if I slapped him real hard.

God, I had never been one to condone violence, but just this once…just really hard…

"You're obnoxious, you know?" I said.

"Yeah. I get that one a lot."

I shook my head, and, at last, his smile died.

"Okay." He sighed. "How about this, I need you to believe me. Is that better?"

I frowned. "If that's your attempt at saying sorry and at worming your way back into my trust, you're wasting your time. You know why they say never trust a liar? You lie once, you lie again, and before you realize it, you have created a whole bunch of them, not knowing what's true and not, and it all goes down the drain, because no one believes them anymore. Tell me one good reason why I should believe you, Chase?"

"Point well taken," he said. "I admit I don't deserve your trust. I married you for selfish reasons. I can't deny it started that way, but now—" He paused, letting the last word linger heavy in the air. "—*now* that we're married, I want a chance to explain."

I shook my head, my head reeling from his words.

"Wow," I said at last. "You're unbelievable. That's the shittiest reason I've ever heard."

"I know."

I looked up to meet a glint of amusement in his eyes. His face was clean-shaven, his mouth soft. His lips looked deliciously kissable. My pulse sped up at the thought of kissing him for the sake of it. Just to be close to him one more time.

His lips twitched and his gaze lingered on my mouth for a bit too long, as though he could read my thoughts and had a few of his own.

I sighed. "Chase, when I say you're unbelievable, it's not a compliment. What you did is despicable."

God.

What was it with this guy and his ego?

"I know," he said again. "I wouldn't be here if it wasn't. So, do you want an explanation or what?" Judging from the way his fingers tapped on his thigh impatiently, it really had to be important.

I shrugged. "There's no point in fighting it anymore."

"No, there isn't. Not if you don't want me pestering you for the rest of your life." He gave a short laugh and his fingers brushed mine, the motion sending a jolt of pleasure through me. "Come on, birdie, we're late."

"Late for what?"

"Just go with it."

"Fine." I sighed, already hating the fact that I was caving in.

***

We left the hotel. The sun was still high on the horizon, and it was insanely hot. My damp hair dried in minutes, and a layer of sweat covered my skin. I fought the urge to tie my hair at the back of my nape as I followed Chase to a string of shiny cars.

At first, I didn't realize what was happening, until a man standing in front of a black Lincoln Stretch Limousine greeted Chase and opened the doors for us.

My jaw dropped.

Oh, my God.

I stopped in mid-stride.

"What now?" Chase turned to face me and gave an exasperated sigh.

"I said I'm giving you a chance to explain." I gestured at the car and the driver. "I never agreed to a date."

"I know that." He grinned. "But why shouldn't we have some fun in a smooth ride while I get to explain?"

"Fun?" I raised my eyebrows.

I didn't want fun. I wanted an explanation or at least some form of proof that Chase wasn't the bad boy I imagined him to be. Another limousine pulled in. The driver threw an anxious glance at Chase, muttering something in Spanish I didn't understand.

"It's bulletproof and safe," Chase said when he caught my expression. "Come on, baby. We're in the way."

His hands moved to the small of my back—his fingers warm against the thin material barely covering my skin— and he helped me in. Before I knew it, the doors closed behind us. I was about to ask him to let me out when I turned around to scan our surroundings.

"Oh, my god," I exclaimed, overwhelmed.

Wow.

Talk about huge. Talk about awesome.

The limousine was much bigger than I anticipated and completely modern. While I used to travel in luxurious cars when I was a kid, and having a chauffeur wasn't new to me, I had never been in a limousine. It could easily host a whole party of ten, or twelve, or fifteen.

There was even a mirrored, illuminated bar with crystal decanters and wine glasses, and at the farther end of the cabin there were two mounted LCD TVs. The gray carpet under my feet looked soft, urging me to pull off my shoes and bury my naked feet into the plush fabric. The expensive, cream, leather seats looked comfortable enough to snuggle up with a good book.

Even from where I was half-standing, half-hunched, I could smell the scent of the expensive leather. At the rear end of the cabin more bottles of wine and wine glasses were stacked on a side rack next to an aquarium. I took a seat next to it and peered around.

"You like it?" Chase's voice said behind me as the limousine began to move.

"It's okay." I shrugged, trying not to look too impressed. He had outdone himself—maybe a little too much.

Because he wants something.

"They're Siamese fighting fish," Chase said casually, and I realized I had been staring at the fish.

"Beautiful," I said and sighed.

Above us, the mirror ceiling shimmered in an array of nuances, giving the impression of a starry sky. As if on cue, the color changed from a beautiful emerald green to a royal blue.

"Red or white?" Chase asked and began to busy himself at the bar. His handsome face looked even more gorgeous under the blue light.

"Red."

"Red it is." He pulled a bottle of red wine from the minibar and poured two glasses. I realized the bottle had already been opened. Was it my imagination or had Chase known my choice even before I answered, or why else would he have opened the bottle to let it breathe?

"I never agreed to this, you know?" I said casually as he handed me a wine glass and sat down opposite from me, his knee brushing mine in the process.

Of all the places where he could have sat, why did he have to choose the seat next to mine?

"Relax, Laurie. It's just a ride I booked for the day."

"For the day?" I stared at him. "Chase."

He cast me a sideways glance and grinned slyly. "I promise you'll have fun."

The fun part again.

My body heated up as images of him touching me flooded my mind.

Was it wrong to want him?

Behind tinted windows and within the confined space.

Under the starry sky, and to the sound of bubbling water.

Actually, why did those things so important that they occupied my mind more than my initial plan to find out what he was up to?

Because I wanted to touch him, kiss him, have him inside me. I wanted to repeat the experience that had left me panting his name.

As if sensing my thoughts, Chase's gaze brushed my mouth. My lips tingled from the memory of his heated kisses.

My heart fluttered and my heart rate spiked up.

I had to change the topic before I did something stupid and he noticed just how much he had gotten under my skin.

"Is that why you wanted me to wear the red dress?" I asked quietly, turning my attention to my glass.

"No, I was actually pining for the blue one you're wearing." His words surprised me and I looked up again. He took a sip of his wine, his eyes never leaving mine.

"What?"

"I knew you'd choose the blue one if I so much as mentioned the red one. Plus, it's my favorite color." He winked at me. "It's been ever since I saw you in your little nightshirt."

He always knew what to say—that ability had been my downfall.

My throat choked up. The nervous bundle inside my stomach was back with a vengeance. My skin burned.

Back at the hotel, I'd had a sip or two of alcohol. Now I felt as though I needed an entire bottle. It was the effect Chase had on me. He made me nervous, more so after what had happened between us. The fact that he was sitting so close to me made it all even worse.

Meeting with him was a mistake.

Just looking at him in his blue jeans and white shirt was painful.

He was too beautiful a reminder of what I couldn't have.

"Why couldn't you give your explanation at the hotel?" I asked.

Where I felt safe; where I could have walked away easily.

"Because this is my treat," he replied. "I wanted to do something nice for you."

I sighed. "I don't want a treat, Chase. I want an explanation. It's the only reason I agreed to this."

"And you'll get one."

So he kept saying.

"When?" I asked.

He gestured at my glass, and I took another sip. "Can

we have lunch first? You look like you haven't eaten yet."

He was right.

"Why do you care?"

He shrugged. "Because you're my wife?"

"Fake wife," I corrected, adding softly, "The target of your deception, in case you've forgotten."

He wet his lips, his blue eyes darkening as he glanced down at his glass, the dark liquid swirling, reflecting the changing lights above.

I don't know what I expected, but disappointment washed over me. Somehow, I thought he'd tell me that I was wrong, but he didn't say anything. Worse yet, the way he avoided my gaze told me that I was more than right.

"So you don't deny it?" I asked.

"Please, Laurie, not now," he said softly. "Can we have lunch first and then talk?"

I bit on my lower lip, considering whether to push him. With my stomach growling, and still feeling tired and weak, I wasn't even sure I had the strength to discuss Chase's intentions. I had no clue what his plans were or where they would leave me. I had no idea if my instinct to run stood a chance against my feelings for him, and that scared me. I didn't want to go to that one place, where I became a blindly trusting idiot.

"Where are we going?" I asked, my fingers playing with the glass.

"You'll see soon enough." He cast me a strange glance. "What? Are you bored already? Or don't you trust me?"

I shrugged. "I don't see what the big deal is. You understand this is no date?"

"Yes, I heard you loud and clear," he said and placed his empty glass back on the bar. "It just isn't the ideal place for it, that's all."

"Yeah?" I frowned. "And what's the place you envisioned?"

"One that serves seafood."

"Seafood?" I let out a brief laugh, surprised by his answer.

"If life gives you crap, then the only cure is crab."

He laughed and leaned back. "I was kidding."

"It wasn't funny."

"I thought it was." His lips twitched. "You're not allergic to seafood, are you?" He leaned closer and draped his arm around my shoulders, not waiting for my answer. "No, you aren't. See, that's the beauty of our relationship. I know everything about you thanks to your very detailed info leaflet you sent me."

I pushed his arm away. "First, we don't have a relationship, Chase."

"That's right. We're married. There's a difference."

"No...yes. Call it whatever you want, it's over. Not to mention, it was fake," I said annoyed. "And second, I only sent you my detailed biography because you asked me for one."

"Thank you for that. It's helped me understand the complexity of your soul." He tipped his nose with his finger.

My soul?

His charm was working, and it pissed me off.

"Good for you," I said, my annoyance rising to new heights. "I still have no idea who you are. I'm not even sure why I'm playing along—" I waved my hand around as I struggled to find the right words "—here when I should be thousands of miles away, thanking my lucky stars that it's all over."

"Would it help you if you saw some proof of identification?" Chase asked.

Definitely couldn't hurt.

My breath caught in my throat. "Is that a joke?"

"I'm dead serious." Not waiting for my reply, he pulled out his wallet from his jean pocket and tossed it to me. It fell straight into my lap. I stared at the beaten, brown leather, then glanced up at him, unsure what to do.

"Come on," Chase said, watching me. "Take it before you go and accuse me of stealing someone's identity."

I let out a laugh. "As if stealing someone's identity could top stealing someone's money. It's just as bad, but definitely not worse."

His hand touched mine. I pulled back.

"Laurie, I'm not after your money," he insisted. His anger was palpable in his tone. "Besides, one quarter of your inheritance is not exactly a lot." My eyes widened at his statement.

Judging from the car he drove and the place he owned, he wasn't exactly poor.

"Yeah, I read your file. I know the terms of your inheritance, and what you wanted to agree to." His finger tapped on the wallet. "Come on. Have a look. We'll be a step closer to where I want us to be after you do."

He sounded so forceful I couldn't help but feel hopeful.

My fingers shook as I grabbed the wallet from my lap. As I opened it, my eyes fell on the countless credit cards and then on his driver's license.

I pulled it out, swallowing down the lump in my throat.

Chase Wright.

Even his date of birth was correct, and the guy in the picture was definitely Chase, albeit a younger version of him.

Confusion washed over me.

I didn't know what I had expected. That maybe it would all be fake—just like our marriage. I most certainly didn't expect that he might be telling the truth.

He moved closer to me, his lips almost touching my ear. "Did you really think I would marry you with a fake name?

How exactly would that have worked out?"

"I'm not sure." I turned my head to him and took a sip of my wine, then another until my glass was empty, but the much-desired numbing effect didn't kick in.

"I was born in Texas, Mulberry, which you already know." He stashed the driver's license back in his wallet when he caught my expression of disbelief. "What? Not everything I told you was a lie."

"Like your acting?"

"I'm not an actor per se," he said. "But I did act when I was younger."

"You did?" I couldn't hold back a snort.

"Mmm. You think I would go to all the trouble of setting up several fake profiles? I don't have time for that."

"As a matter of fact, I think you'd do just that, Chase." His name sounded so right on my lips, I winced. We were married for real. No doubt about that now. The thought both scared and excited me. "In fact, I think you'd go the extra mile to meet me."

He thought it over for a moment. "I did go through quite a bit to meet you."

Like committing arson, trapping us in an elevator, and hurting a lot of people.

It was such a long time ago that it all felt like a bad dream.

That minuscule smidgen of despair intermingled with

hope was back again.

I opened my mouth to speak when the car stopped and Chase grabbed my hand again, giving it a little squeeze. "We're here."

"Where's here?"

"The shore," he said the exact moment the driver opened the door. "There's nothing better than a bit of sunshine, wine, and—" He grinned. "Say it."

"Crabs."

"That's right. Crabs." He grimaced. "Unless you get the bad kind. Now that makes one's life kind of bad."

I turned my head away from him, my lips twitching.

Would it be so bad if I laughed?

Argh.

He was making it so difficult not to like him.

Biting my lip, I chuckled inwardly as I followed him out, inhaling the distinct smell of salt, water, and seafood.

Chapter 12

THE RESTAURANT WAS situated on top of a hill
overlooking the sea. I expected it to be secluded. However,
it was overcrowded with people and families. Mexican
folklore music was playing in the background, and children
were laughing. I turned to Chase questioningly, but he only
grinned, as a waiter approached us.

All around us, people were eating, chatting, and having a
great time. It was so busy and overcrowded that I was
convinced the waiter would tell us they were overbooked,
until he led us through a doorway to an open patio. I held
my breath, amazed, as we followed him to a table near the
railing.

Coming here was a mistake.

The place was beautiful. *Too beautiful.* Too perfect for something that should have been a day of enlightenment, not romance, happiness, and perfection.

I slid into the seat, unable to pull my eyes away from the stunning scenery. Even though it wasn't quiet, the place was pure tranquility. It was a place I could imagine myself sitting for hours, drinking coffee and relaxing to the sound of the crashing waves. If only the situation wasn't so awkward. If only Chase and I were a real couple.

Somewhere a child shrieked, and a thought occurred to me.

"Did you choose a public restaurant so that I wouldn't make a scene?" I asked. "If so, I can tell you that your fears were unwarranted. I'm not one of those girls who cause tantrums. I have a very good grasp on my emotions."

"I know that." He sat opposite from me with an easy smile on his lips. "You're one of those girls who choose flight over confrontation. Am I right?"

"True." I nodded as I eyed him warily. "You didn't answer my question, Chase."

"No, it's not the reason we're here." He leaned back, watching me in thought. "I've been told it's the best place in town with a stunning view, as you can see."

"And?" I prompted after a pause.

"And it's safe and secure."

"You mean for you," I asked, raising my eyebrows.

"No, I mean for you, Laurie." Was it my imagination or was there more to it?

I frowned. "What do you mean?"

"I want you to feel safe in my presence, considering you ran away."

I stared at him.

Safe from Chase?

Confusion washed over me until realization hit me.

He thought I had fled because I was scared.

"That's not the reason I ran away, Chase," I said coolly. "I'm not afraid of you."

"You're not?" He seemed surprised, as though any other explanation wouldn't make sense. And then he leaned forward, his eyes taking me in. "I thought you felt scared because you thought I'd hurt you." I shook my head, meeting his warm glance with a cold stare. "Then why, Laurie?"

"I…" I flicked my tongue over my lips, unsure how to say it.

Was I scared that I'd get hurt? Probably.

But not in a physical sense.

I was scared of having my heart broken more than he had already broken it. Of never being able to pick up the pieces he left behind. Of hoping for something that would never be there—his love, his devotion.

"Because of what you discovered?" he insisted.

135

"Yes. That's probably one of the reasons." I stared at my hands fiddling on the table, and his hand, so close to my fingers, beckoning to me to grab it. "The other one is…"

I thought you were really into me.

I thought what we had was real.

"You really fucking hurt me," I said instead, speaking out the truth before I could stop it.

The words lingered in the air, heavy, real.

He glanced down at his hands, guilt flashing across his face. And suddenly his whole body tensed. "For what it's worth, I really like you, Laurie. And…" He leaned forward and grabbed my hand, his eyes on me, begging me to understand a message only he knew. "…if things were different, if I didn't have to do what I've done, I would have asked you out."

If things were different, if I didn't have to do what I've done…

I laughed, his words echoing in my mind.

I eyed his fingers on mine, caressing my skin, and fought the sudden urge to pull back.

"So let me see if I understand," I whispered. "You married me for my inheritance."

"Yes," he said cautiously. "But I also like you." He let the words linger in the air. "If things were different, I would still want to date you."

"Why?" I asked, my voice breathless.

"Simply because. Do you need a reason for it?"

My breath hitched as I regarded him. The wind blew my hair into my face, and I pushed the strand behind my ear. His eyes softened.

"What? Is that really so hard to believe that I might be developing feelings for you?" Chase asked.

There, he had just said it. All of a sudden, my world began to spin.

"I don't know." I swallowed. "It's hard to believe. I've been… I don't think—"

God, what was happening to me?

I couldn't finish sentences whenever he was around.

"Laurie." He breathed out an impatient sigh. "You're beautiful. Why is it hard to believe that I like you?"

Because I'm nothing like you.

"I'm not confident. I'm not…" I struggled for words.

Perfect.

Godlike.

God, I had to stop before it got out of control. There was something about his penetrating stare that threw me off. Or maybe it was his touch—gently and warm, and completely out of place—that my whirling thoughts couldn't formulate one single sentence. Whatever it was, it had to stop.

Withdrawing my hand from him, I took a deep breath and let it out slowly.

"You don't have to be confident," he replied. "I like you

for who you are."

"Why did you marry me?" I asked. My question was meant to be casual. Instead, it came out like an accusation.

There was a long pause.

"Because I had to," he said at last.

There was something in his voice: hope that I would believe him. Hope that I would forgive him even though his words were the painful beginning of a longer story. I scanned his face and saw the despair etched in his features.

"Is it because of the money?" I asked.

"No." He shook his head, his frown deepening, and I knew, whatever the answer, whatever explanation he would give me, I wouldn't like the truth. And he knew it. He knew I knew, judging from the way he couldn't even look me straight in my eyes, and kept delaying the inevitable.

Everything inside me burned with the knowledge that if he had wanted, he could have disclosed his reasons back at the hotel.

That he didn't, that he couldn't do it now, didn't just bother me.

It confirmed to me that whatever he had to say was going to be difficult—for both of us.

Heck, I wasn't sure I was ready to hear it.

The entire situation was worse than facing my stepfather.

It was splitting me into two.

"I wish things could be different," he said and turned his attention to the ocean. I did the same as I let go of my thoughts and *him*.

Sitting so close to the railing overlooking the shore, the sight was beautiful. The blue water stood in contrast to the sand, my dark feelings and the despair that seemed to rise within me, reminding me that this was only a fleeting moment in our lives.

Everything felt surreal—the sparkling water, the warm sun on our faces, the excited chatter all around us. For a moment, it felt as though it wasn't my life, but someone else's.

"It doesn't matter anymore. I'm—" My words were interrupted by a waitress stopping at our table.

"Quiere algo para beber?" the waitress asked.

I looked into her friendly face, ready to ask whether she could speak English. But Chase replied.

"You can speak Spanish?" I asked after she left.

"I wish I were fluent," he said. "But I only throw in bits of phrases here and there to impress."

As if he needed to impress when his body already did the work for him.

"Have you been here before?" I asked warily.

"No." He leaned forward, his eyes watching me with renewed interest. "What was it that you wanted to say before you were interrupted? You said that it doesn't matter anymore."

He had been listening. I didn't expect that. "I can't remember."

It was a lie.

But he couldn't know the truth.

It doesn't matter anymore. I'm already in love with you.

Chase was a weakness I couldn't have in my life. My feelings for him would always make me an easy target.

I might be gullible, but I wasn't weak. Before I could change the topic, the waitress arrived with several plates. As she spread out the varied delicacies and arranged the plates in what seemed to be a specific order, I stared in surprise at the array of food.

I raised my brows at Chase and he smiled, the skin around his eyes crinkling.

"I took the liberty to order and paid for it before we came," he clarified. "This place can be quite busy. I didn't want to keep you waiting."

"You didn't have to," I said and helped myself to a plate.

"It was my pleasure. Can't afford to disappoint my wife. What are you having?"

His wife.

As if.

His words had me blushing, so I scanned the seafood. There was so much of everything, it looked like someone had prepared an entire dinner table for a dinner party rather than for just the two of us.

Everything looked so delicious I didn't know where to start.

"No idea. Maybe everything?" I said.

"Try this." He picked up a shrimp taco and held it up to my mouth. "It's spicy."

I laughed. "My stomach won't tolerate it."

"The taste is worth the stomach pain."

I laughed again, realizing he acted as if nothing had happened between us, even though everything had changed. I stared at him, my heart plummeting as I became aware of how intimate the entire situation was—and how close he had come to tricking my mind into thinking that we could go on with our lives, never talking about what happened.

"Fine. But you'll wish you had tried it," he said.

My laugh died on my lips as I watched Chase withdraw his hand and bite into the taco. He took a napkin and wiped off his hands, nodding appreciatively.

"Chase." I sighed. "Why are you doing this?"

"What? Taking you out for lunch?" he asked. "I'm treating you nicely. It's the least I can do for you after…" he trailed off, leaving the rest unspoken.

"I meant *this*." I motioned to the air between us. "Acting like nothing happened."

He shrugged. "I'm making a fresh start."

I let the thought sink in for a moment. Grabbing a fork, I started to pop food into my mouth, barely registering the taste.

"You haven't even started to explain your motives, and you already expect me to give you a second chance?" I asked casually. "Wake up, Chase. It's not going to happen. It won't work out."

"It won't work out that I spill my motives, or it won't work out between us?"

Argh.

What was it with this man and his inability to keep a conversation on track?

"Both, obviously," I said dryly.

"I was just asking," he said.

"I thought it was all pretty clear."

"Not to me." He moved his chair to sit closer to me. "You mind?"

I did.

Very much.

The last thing I needed from him was to touch me. To fool me. To remind me that things weren't over—not in my heart anyway.

"Go ahead." I shrugged, as though his proximity didn't faze me.

"I didn't plan this," he started. "I didn't plan to like you, Laurie. You see, in my line of work, you have to be hard

142

and unattached."

"Work?" I asked slowly, my pulse speeding up. "What line of work are we talking about?"

God, my heart was beating real hard. I popped another shrimp into my mouth as I considered his words.

Hard and unattached.

Jude already said that Chase was no actor, so what was he?

Somehow, I couldn't imagine Chase being anything but an actor. Even a porn star would do. Or maybe he was a criminal who had to stay away from all emotional entanglements.

On a second thought, he probably *was* a crook, considering...

"Law," he said casually, interrupting my thoughts.

My breath hitched, and suddenly I had the terrible vision of me choking on a shrimp and that he'd have to perform the Heimlich while everyone was watching, maybe even cheering for him. And then he'd save my life, and I'd owe him for all eternity.

For real.

"What did you say?" I had never felt so faint in my life.

He wiped his fingers on his napkin, then fished out his wallet to retrieve a business card, which he slid across the table toward me.

"I'm a lawyer, Laurie," he said matter-of-factly.

"You're a fucking lawyer?" I asked agog, staring at his card.

Of course, that made sense. If someone knew how to pull a stunt like he had while playing within the constraints of the law, then definitely someone who *knew* the law.

"*Your* lawyer."

My heart skidded to a halt. He leaned forward, whispering, "Or how else do you think I was able to bail you out, all without a trial?"

He had a good point. All of a sudden, I could imagine him in there, asking for evidence, talking about my rights. Oh my god, he probably *was* really good at it.

Sexy as hell in his tailored suit and with those burning eyes.

A lawyer!

Who would have thought?

A man of the law. Someone to fight for justice. And he tricked me into marrying him.

For selfish reasons.

Without meaning to, I started to laugh, the onset of hysteria bubbling at the back of my throat.

"What's so funny?" His voice was still calm, but carried the slightest hint of irritation.

"You, my fake, lying, husband, reading my rights as my lawyer and talking about the law and justice."

"It also helped when I stated that we were newlyweds,"

he said with a frown on his beautiful face as he watched me. "I also told them you got so wasted you didn't know what you were doing."

"Are you fucking kidding me, Chase?" I shook my head, my laugh dying in my throat. "Did you not hear a word I said? I don't give a shit how you got me out." Anger started to pour out of me in long, thick waves. "I can't believe you're a lawyer. A man of the law. Out of all professions, this one is about the most unsuitable you could have picked."

I took a sip of my wine. Then a few more as a tear ran down my face. I wiped it away angrily.

"Laurie?" he said taken aback. "I know how this looks," he said again for the umpteenth time of the day.

"No. Let's not go there again." I put the empty glass down, and then looked up to his face. "Let me sum it up, Chase. You planned all this?"

"Yes." He nodded.

"And you learned all about sticking to the truth with an oath and all that shit?"

He closed his eyes and whispered, "Yes."

"And you married me for real?"

"I think we've established that already."

"For your own selfish reasons."

He took his time with a reply. "Yes."

"How do you lawyers call it?" I asked a little too

forcefully. "It's called fraud, Chase. It's fucking against the law to marry someone based on ulterior motivations."

He said nothing.

"You've just corrupted the law you should be believing in," I said flatly. "It would make so much sense if you told me you were an assassin."

He cocked an eyebrow. "Seriously, Laurie? You're being dramatic."

"Am I?" I prompted. "The whole situation is dramatic. It's fucking ridiculous." I threw the napkin on the table, fighting the urge to walk away and never see him again. "I'm leaving."

His fingers curled around mine with enough pressure to keep me frozen in place. "Don't." I watched his grip on me. He followed my line of vision and loosened his grip a little. "Please," he said softly.

"Okay."

"It's not as a bad as you make it out to be," Chase said.

"It's not?" I smiled bitterly. "You were there on that day the floor crashed." My voice broke. "You hurt all those people. And you're saying it's not a big deal? How could you do that?"

His eyes widened as shock flashed across his face.

"Come on, Laurie. You know me." He sounded genuinely upset. "I didn't hurt anyone."

"Chase, I saw the folder. I saw the evidence that you

146

were involved."

"I wasn't responsible for it," he said again, this time his tone was harsh and brisk—like a whiplash. "Look, I might be a liar, and I most certainly broke a few laws by marrying you for a reason, but I'm not a killer."

"I saw the folder," I repeated. "You knew when to meet me."

"Yes." He nodded.

"So," I cut him off, the words evading me. "You were responsible for the fire."

His eyes narrowed. "I see what would make you think that, but honestly, you're way off the radar."

"Am I?"

"Very." He closed his eyes for a second, then opened them again as he inhaled deeply. "I'd never do something like that."

"How do I know you're telling me the truth?"

"Because that's my work. I know those people."

"How's that your work?" I asked, confused.

"LiveInvent is a client. I come in at least once a week. I have business lunches with those people. We go out for drinks."

My mouth went dry.

"You represent LiveInvent?" My voice came out too loud, and a few people turned their heads toward us. "Sorry," I mouthed and cleared my throat.

"Yes," Chase said, composed as usual.

"So…" I shook my head to make sense of it all. "You didn't know I was coming in that day?"

"Actually, I did. That's the thing, Laurie," he said quietly. "In fact, I made sure you got that interview, and if that floor hadn't collapsed, you would have been invited to attend a second interview, after which you would have gotten the job. But after what happened, you ignored all calls and invitations to attend another interview. What was I supposed to do to get to meet you, except befriend Jude on Facebook?"

He was right.

After the whole floor crashed, LiveInvent followed up with an email, another invitation to an interview, but I didn't respond. They even called to tell me how much they wanted to meet me because they really believed I'd be suited for the job.

I ignored everything because I was scared.

Shock did that to someone.

"Why didn't you come?" Chase asked, interested.

"The whole thing was too much," I said honestly. "Being stuck in an elevator, with no hope of getting out, I was sure it was going to be my last day. I couldn't go back to that place, not when I thought you were dead." I shook my head grimly. "I thought I'd never see you again. I didn't want to be reminded of you."

"You thought I was dead?" he asked quietly.

I nodded silently.

"Remember that I told you everything would be okay?" I nodded again and he continued, "I promised myself that I'd do whatever it took to save you. Well, you're alive."

I don't know why, but my eyes suddenly felt moist again. My throat choked up, and a tear trickled down my cheek.

I looked away, strangely emotional.

There were at least thirty people around us.

Why couldn't Chase choose a less public place? To distract me, to calm myself, I grabbed a shrimp and bit into it. The salty flavor reached my taste buds, but it didn't quite register in my brain.

"So, what are you? A chevalier? A hero?" I asked carefully, unsure what he wanted me to say.

"I would love to say that, but I'm not...as I'm sure you've noticed by now." He began to pile food onto his plate, the motion easing some of the tension between us. "I'm really proud of myself that I once saved a woman's life in an elevator. That's about the grandest thing I've ever done in my life."

He was talking about me, no doubt about that. "You cannot make me feel guilty," I said coldly. "It won't change anything between us."

"That wasn't my intention," Chase said just as coldly.

For a while we sat there in silence. Eventually, Chase began to eat. My stomach rumbled again, reminding me that it would be a pity to waste all that good food. I filled up my own plate and busied myself with my meal. At some point, a waitress appeared with our dessert consisting of two trays with ice cream and tantalizing pastries.

But I couldn't touch them. And neither did Chase.

"Are you finished?" he asked.

I glanced up and met his gaze. His eyes were burning, and I realized with a shock, that it was sadness that I saw in them.

"Yes," I mumbled.

"Then let's go.

Chapter 13

WE'D BEEN BACK in the limousine for only a few minutes, with neither of us speaking, and it already felt like a whole eternity had passed. I was sitting next to the fish tank, my head leaned back against the leather, Chase at the other end, a glass of bourbon in his hand. Neither of us dared to look at each other. Neither of us dared to talk. And I would be damned if I was the first one.

Finally, Chase moved to the bar. At first, I thought it was to refill his glass. Instead, he sat down next to me—far enough to give me privacy, close enough to make my heart race.

"Look, Laurie," he started, rolling the glass between his hands. "I get you are pissed."

I let out a laugh.

"I'm not pissed. I'm hurt. There's a huge difference." I paused as I prepared my words. "I thought you were different, Chase. When I married you and let you fuck me, I thought I knew you. I would never have guessed that all that time you were working on your little folder about me. You didn't even tell me that we had already met a few months ago."

"Fair enough." He took a deep breath. "I'd been watching you for some time. Obviously, I couldn't disclose that fact. Nor the fact that we met the day the floor crashed."

I looked up and met his blue eyes. The way he said it, I was sure he didn't even feel sorry. Heck, I wasn't even sure he had any regrets.

Anger rose inside me.

"You hurt all those people." My voice shook. I didn't try to hide the disgust in my voice.

He shook his head. "No, I didn't do that. That was pure coincidence."

"Coincidence?" I let out another short laugh and leaned forward, eyeing him carefully. I had a hard time believing that one. "I don't believe in coincidences. Only in patterns and habits."

"How would you know that?" His question was cold, just like his gaze. "Do you know what fate has in store for you? Maybe it was destiny for me to meet you. I don't see a pattern in anything about us."

"What are you saying, Chase?"

"The answer's simple," he said. "I wanted to meet you. We arranged for you to attend an interview. On the day we were supposed to meet for the first time, I wanted to make sure that'd you nail the interview, so I got into that elevator with you. That day the floor crashed, and that was a coincidence." He took a sip from his glass, taking his time before he continued. "I didn't mean for that to happen, just like I didn't plan to like you. There are no fixed patterns. Only plans and hope and coincidences, and a whole lot of mistakes that indicate something bigger than us is out here."

Was I the mistake?

I had no idea, but a more important question hovered at the back of my mind.

"Who is 'we'?" I asked.

He frowned. "What?"

"You said '*we* arranged it.' Who's that, Chase?"

"My brother and I."

"That would be Kade?" My question sounded more like a statement. He nodded. "I thought you were an only child."

"Well, you thought wrong."

"Are you sure you're related?" I replied. "You don't look alike at all. Could be another one of your lies."

"Not everything I told you is a lie, Laurie. I think I made myself clear on that one," Chase reminded me softly. His hand moved toward me, and for a moment I thought he might touch me. That he didn't sent a jolt of disappointment through me. "What I'm telling you right now is the truth."

"I wouldn't have it any other way," I mumbled.

"My parents adopted Kade after I was born," Chase said, ignoring my remark. "When they found out they couldn't conceive, but wanted me to grow up with a brother." He raised his eyebrows at my expression. "What? Is that really so hard to believe? You of all people should understand it. Clint adopted you when he married your mom."

I frowned. "You know?"

"I did my research, Laurie," he said dryly. "Obviously, I know."

"It's not the same thing."

"Adopted is adopted. The circumstances don't matter much."

I stared at him in thought, undecided whether to believe him. "Talking about truth and all, did you send your brother to Acapulco to follow me?"

"No." He shook his head. "I told you already that I had absolutely no idea he was here. He didn't tell me."

He looked so earnest, I had no doubt he was telling the

truth—for a change. He also looked pissed, but I didn't care. I crossed my arms over my chest and regarded him to see if his anger would manifest itself in some way. He didn't vent, but then Chase never did, and that was scary.

It would have been easier to believe that he was a good actor rather than a lawyer. Mystery and fantasy were easier pills to swallow than reality. The thought that I might be falling for another one of his tricks turned my stomach to ice.

"I find it very hard to believe you," I said at last. "There's no way you can prove you're not responsible for the fire."

People did all sorts of things for money. He had already added deceit to his résumé, so why not arson?

His lips tightened, and the frown on his forehead deepened. He gave an exasperated, annoyed sigh. "My brother owns LiveInvent. You think he would have let me do that? Is that proof enough for you?"

My heart thudded in my chest. It shouldn't really have been a surprise, and yet it was.

"Look, Laurie." He leaned forward, misinterpreting my expression. "The building had some minor construction problems from the beginning. We were working with an engineer to solve the issues, and the renovation plans were awaiting approval. Everyone thought we had time. The whole thing was a ticking bomb." He shook his head, his eyes dark and gloomy. "Trust me, no one wanted or anticipated that to happen. It just did. It cost Kade a lot of money, and it sure made things difficult for us to get close to you. It also pushed back our plans because we had more pressing issues to deal with."

"What do you mean?"

"It kept the legal department busy for a while. That's when I came up with the idea of befriending Jude." He grabbed the bottle from the bar, filled another glass, then moved back to his seat. The space behind him was black, and I realized it was a partition that could be rolled down to speak to the driver.

For a few seconds, he sat here, the lights above us changing from violet to blue. When he spoke again, his voice was low and wary—as if every word spoken was well prepared. "The original plan was to interview, hire you, then work with you to build up trust," he said. "You had all the qualifications anyway, so it would have worked out."

"After which you wanted me to fall in love with you, and you would have proposed, right?" I asked.

He hesitated, the tip of his tongue flicking across his lips. "That was the plan, yes. Falling in love would have been a necessity."

I let out a sarcastic laugh as another flash of pain rose inside me.

His words hurt, but what wounded me the most was

that he was right. It was such a good plan. I had to give him that.

I would have fallen in love with him, just like any other woman out there. Given that I'd obsessed over a guy in a dark elevator, I would have probably jumped at the idea of dating him.

The truth was, it wasn't hard to fall for Chase. He was sexy, confident, always knew what to say, available.

Too good to be true.

I knew that right from the beginning. I just didn't listen to my intuition and the alarm bells ringing at the back of my mind.

If Chase were the light, I would be his moth, drawn to him even though I know I'll get burned.

Even though I was already burning.

"So, it wouldn't have made a difference if you met me then; the outcome would be the same," I whispered.

"If you put it like that, yes," he replied.

"You didn't need months to make me trust you." My voice quivered. "It took you what? Three weeks? You really did a fantastic job. Well done." I clapped my hands to applaud him. "You should be proud of yourself."

"Please don't do that," he said through gritted teeth.

I threw my hands up in the air. "What? I'm praising your talents. Or are you ashamed? Are you having regrets?" His mouth tightened again, and the nerve under his right eye began to twitch again. Nope. No regrets there. "Thought so," I muttered.

My self-control surprised me, not least because inside I was breaking in places I didn't know I existed.

I would leave Chase with my dignity intact.

That was the plan.

I lifted Chase's half-full glass to my lips and, kicking off my shoes, I leaned back against the leather seat and took a generous sip.

The liquid burned its way down my throat.

If we had to have this conversation, I'd better get some alcohol in me. And fast.

"Why did you really marry me?" I asked casually as I took another sip. "I know it's about money, but you don't look like you need it. Besides, you know I don't have any. And don't tell me it's because you want to help me. We both know that's bullshit."

"I thought you might ask that at some point," he said again, avoiding my eyes. "It does involve your inheritance."

"You said that already," I said, infusing confidence I didn't feel into my voice. "But you also said you weren't interested in my money, and you know damn well I own nothing. So forgive me that I'm confused."

"That's right. I'm not interested in *your* money," he explained. "It's not money *per se* I'm after, but the inheritance Clint gets."

I frowned as my brain began to struggle to put the pieces together.

"Clint?" I asked slowly and leaned forward. Chase nodded. "Why are we talking about him?"

"Because Clint *is* the reason I married you."

Oh, God.

My stomach dropped and my head began to spin.

Suddenly, I felt weak. My grip tightened around the glass, and for a moment I feared it might snap. I stared at Chase shell-shocked. "Did Clint make you do it?"

Sighing, he leaned forward to lift the bottle from the bar, poured himself another glass, then shifted in his seat, his eyes still avoiding me. For the first time something flashed across his face. Judging from the way his expression hardened and his shoulders tensed, he was fuming mad.

"You couldn't be more wrong," he said, his tone dripping with disdain that I thought was addressed at me. "Your stepfather destroyed everything we had. Our home. My family's business. Everything my parents had built in thirty years—all lost in the span of a few weeks." His voice was quiet but firm, every word spoken with so much hatred, it made me flinch. "He ruined us, so it's only fair that I destroy and ruin what is his."

"I don't understand," I said, struggling to find the words as confusion wreaked havoc in my head. "What you're talking about is a personal issue. It's...my God, it's—"

"Revenge." He looked up. I shrank back at the intensity in his glance. "Revenge, Laurie. You were the only way to get close to him, I guess."

My heart started to hammer—fast and hard, just like his words.

I held my breath as I took him in—the way he let the golden liquid swirl in his glass, his face drawn in concentration, as if it took great effort to do so.

He downed his glass before he continued, "When we first heard of you, we thought you had a close relationship with him. I mean, he adopted you."

"I don't have any relationship with him."

"We didn't know that back then," Chase said and shook his head. "He sent you checks every month."

"Which I always sent back," I interrupted.

He shook his head again, as though it didn't matter. "Anyway, we dug deep. We found out that his business is tied to your mom's money, your inheritance, so the plan was to marry you and ruin him." He put the glass away, and slowly turned his whole body to me. He eyed me as if I was an object, not a human being—with cold, calculating eyes that scared the crap out of me.

I had never seen him so detached. So—

Different.

"So what I am to you?" My voice sounded awfully thin. "A pawn in your play? Collateral damage?"

He didn't reply.

Worse yet, he started to bite his lower lip. In the short time I had known Chase, I had learned that it meant whatever I'd just said was true, though he wouldn't admit it.

Piece by piece of me began to crumble to bits. My throat closed up. The confined space felt devoid of air.

We had no future. None whatsoever.

My lips began to quiver. I swallowed hard, over and over again. I wasn't going to give him the satisfaction of seeing me cry over him.

Stupid me.

All that time, I had thought Chase cared for me. Even after finding the folder, my heart came up with bullshit excuses—him being in trouble, involved with the wrong kind of people, needing money.

Never in my wildest dreams had I envisioned that I had been targeted because of something my stepfather had done. That it might all be a ploy to get revenge.

In a deep corner of my mind, I recalled tiny morsels of conversation between Clint and his lawyer I had often overheard. As a child I had always assumed they were talking about won trials, boasting about the things they had done and all the money they had taken.

I had realized a long time ago that Clint wasn't who he pretended to be. I wasn't sure what to think anymore, but I was inclined to believe that Chase was probably one of the people Clint and Aldwin had harmed.

Clint had many enemies, so why wouldn't Chase be one of them? It was impossible to like someone like Clint who stopped at nothing to further his own gain.

Greed did that to people. And Clint was as sneaky as was humanly possible. When he first met my mom, he was a car salesman with the necessary character traits to make it big—manipulative and passive-aggressive—two qualities he managed to nourish in the following years.

Looking at Chase, I realized maybe they had that in common.

"You said your inheritance isn't worth anything to you," Chase said, interrupting my thoughts. "If that's really the case, it all doesn't matter. It's a marriage of convenience. You wanted the letters, and I want revenge. What's so hard to accept?"

The way he put it—cold and cruel, as if we were talking about a business transaction rather than my family; as if nothing had happened between us, and I was only a random encounter in his long list of women—I felt like slapping him.

Maybe you were like a random encounter, Hanson. Easily forgotten.

My heart began to bleed. If he could have seen inside, he would have seen all the blood seeping out of me. There were cracks here and there, little pieces chipping away, and large fragments crumbling to bits. My throat closed up. The air felt devoid of oxygen.

We had no future.

The realization hit me hard.

None whatsoever.

I knew it all along, but had pushed it to the back of my mind. Now I had no other choice but to face the truth.

And it hurt like hell.

"I thought you wanted to help me." My voice broke so I cleared my throat to get rid of the stinging sensation inside. "I never thought you had your own agenda. I thought you cared about me. That's all."

"I do."

"No, you don't." I smiled bitterly and shook my head. "You used me." A silent sob remained lodged in my throat. "You didn't care if I got hurt, Chase," I whispered. Tears began to gather in the corners of my eyes again.

I didn't want to cry and yet I knew I couldn't stop the tears that would soon fall.

"I need your inheritance to destroy him, Laurie." Even though his voice was quiet and steady, I could hear the plea in his tone.

"At my expense," I stated the obvious.

Chase reached for my hand, but I leaned back, pulling it out of his reach.

"Admit it," I said angrily, the pain inside me sharp and

raw. "You wanted revenge at my expense. Just say it. We both know it's the truth."

He took his time to reply, hesitating, as though his silence would make it all less real.

"It needed to be done," he said slowly. "Even if I weren't a part of this, even if things didn't turn out the way they did between us, my brother would have made his move on you. It was either Kade or I."

He made it sound like it was a positive thing. Like I could be passed around. Like I should be grateful it was he and not Kade.

The thought hurt me more than I cared to admit.

I had never felt so insulted in my life.

"So, it was either you or he," I repeated, laughing darkly as I remembered how close I had been to going out with his brother. "Boy, I'm so spoiled with choice." I grimaced. "Doesn't Kade know we got married or why else would he be following me?"

Chase sighed and ran his hand through his silky hair. "I haven't told him."

I frowned. "Why not?"

He closed his eyes, his fingers pressing the bridge of his close. When he opened them again, his expression was hard. His eyes looked like stones, tearing down my wall. I could feel his hate for Clint seeping into my soul. "It's not personal, Laurie. If you just tried to understand why I did it then—"

"Then what?" I cut him off. "I'd see your point? Trust you more?" I shook my head, ignoring the little voice inside my heart that begged me to give him a chance. "I'm sorry, but I didn't sign up for this."

I clutched my bag and squeezed into my shoes. "The conversation's over. I'm not listening to you anymore. Tell the driver to stop the car."

"No, I need you to listen," he said calmly.

But I couldn't. "Let me out, Chase."

"We'll be at the hotel in a few minutes."

"I want to leave now!"

His lips tightened. "Laurie, you don't even know where you are."

"That's not your problem," I said harsher than intended. "Stop the car, Chase."

"Please," Chase said softly. "I can't let you go before you understand."

"Trust me, you were very clear when you said everything you did was out of revenge. What more is there to explain?" He remained silent. I nodded. "Exactly. There's no point in wasting each other's time. Now tell the driver to stop the car."

When Chase didn't move, I turned around and leaned over the seat to hammer against the divider in the hope the driver would hear me. "Stop the car."

"The driver doesn't speak English," Chase said. His voice was calm, but I could hear the slightest hint of desperation in his tone. "Besides, I instructed him not to stop, no matter what happens. I'm afraid you'll have to listen to me for a few more minutes."

I stopped the hammering and turned to face him, my face a mask of fury. "You have no right to hold me here."

"No, I don't. That's why I'm asking." His response surprised me. "Please, Laurie, you haven't heard it all. This is important. It involves our future."

Not my future.

Our future.

"We don't have a future," I said dryly.

Even if I wanted to.

Even if I had believed it at some point.

"Believe it or not, we do have one. According to the contract, we have at least twelve months together."

I let out a sarcastic laugh again.

That damn stupid contract.

That mistake was going to haunt me forever.

Chapter 14

IF I HAD known that Chase was such a pain in the ass, I would never have hired him. Full stop. The first time I'd seen him, I thought he was going to shake my world. Well, he shook my world, rocked it, and made sure that everything I had known and believed in, crashed and burned.

"I'm still the same man, Laurie. I never meant to do you any harm," Chase said, oblivious to my thoughts.

I snorted.

He had never wanted to.

Of course it hadn't been his damn intention.

As if the knowledge would make me feel better.

When people said 'I never meant to do you any harm,'

what they really wanted to say was 'I never meant to do you any harm, but things turned out differently, and there was a choice: you or me. Guess what? You lost."

"I should never have believed you," I whispered. "It was stupid to trust you when you so clearly only think of yourself." I felt the pressure of my unshed tears gathering behind my eyes.

Stupid emotions.

Why couldn't I stop them?

He set his glass down. Instead of replying straight away, he moved closer to me, but didn't touch me.

"I'm not doing it only for myself," he whispered after a pause. "I'm also doing it for you. Why do you think my brother doesn't know we got married?"

"You already said you married me because of your personal issue with Clint," I said matter-of-factly. "As for Kade, maybe you didn't tell him because you were waiting for the surprise party."

His eyebrows rose slightly. "Don't be ridiculous. I'm not just having *issues* with Clint, as you so eloquently put it. It goes much deeper than that." He patted the seat next to him, his voice rising up a notch. "Sit down. This will take at least twenty minutes."

I didn't move. "Ten minutes. Tops. And I'm standing."

"Fine. I'll give you the short version then." He motioned at a nearby seat. When I made no attempt to move, he sighed.

"Guys like Clint pave the way so people like us wind up with nothing," he started. "He used your mother's money—money he was never supposed to touch—to set up a corporation. He uses the funds as loans to small businesses in return for shares knowing that they can't afford to pay back the loans. Then he seemingly helps them so that the business takes off. It all comes down to the business owner not being able to repay him, so he takes over the business and everything else to get his money. That's what happened to a lot of families. This is the simplified version. Basically, many people have lost their income. Their homes. Their dreams. Someone needs to stop him. That someone has to be me."

I ran my tongue across my parched lips, his words resonating in my mind.

Holding my bag in front of me as if it was some shield, I sat down, eyeing him carefully. "So, he supports them in order to cheat them out of their livelihood?"

"I wouldn't call that support. He sets them up for their own fail."

I frowned at his choice of words, my heart racing. "I don't understand. How does he do it?"

"It's all a bit of a gamble," Chase said. "He lends them a lump sump of money and convinces them to invest their money, their homes, everything they own into their business. When things start to go well, he makes sure that a competitor beats them in a series of events that leaves them in greater debt than before, unable to fight him. I don't have to tell you that he's the competitor. His loss is minimal, but the rewards are huge. In the end, Clint is the one who owns the business and all the money invested in it while the previous business owner is left with insurmountable debt."

I frowned. "Is that even legal?"

"Is tricking someone into buying a car that is a piece of shit, legit? Yeah, it is. Unfortunately." He stretched out his legs, an angry expression flashing across his face. "Clint is the reason why I became a lawyer," he continued. "For as long as I can remember, I wanted to be part of the law so guys like him could be served justice. I want to fight; I want to implement a change. Unfortunately, what he does is legal. In the legal sense, all parties involved agreed to his contract. There's absolutely no proof that what he does is premeditated. Without that proof, an investigation is a waste of time."

"He's using the gray area of the legal system to further his own agenda. Just like you did with me," I couldn't help but comment.

"Just like me, yes." He grimaced. "Except, my plan doesn't involve stealing your money or making you lose everything. Actually, quite the contrary's the case. I'm making sure that Clint doesn't get your inheritance," he said. "I never intended to keep it. You have to believe me."

I exhaled a sharp breath.

"Like I said before, I'm not interested in your money," Chase continued. "I want revenge."

"How are you going to accomplish that?"

"As your husband, I can take him to court. Your mother's money is your family heirloom. It belongs to you. He had no right to take and invest it. Just give me a year to sort it out, and he'll be ruined."

I frowned and let out a shaky breath I didn't know I had been holding. At some point, knots of unease had formed in the pit of my stomach. "Are you saying that you'll take him to court? A real trial?"

"It'd involve a little detour, but basically, yes. The plan's to make sure he loses the inheritance, the home that should be yours, everything."

"Oh, my god." I shook my head, closing my eyes.

Fighting my stepfather in court was the last thing I wanted—or needed.

The past few years, I had done my best to stay away from Clint, minimizing contact, forgetting the past. Now that I was married, Chase was trying to force me to face my past again.

I wasn't afraid of Clint. I despised him. I resented him, blamed him for my mother's suicide.

"Once I take everything away from Clint and expose him for who he is, I can return everything that is rightfully yours."

"Aren't you even asking if I want this?" I said weakly.

His brows shot up. "Well, don't you?"

"No, I don't."

My words rendered him silent for a minute.

"You won't have a choice, Laurie," he said coldly. "I'm your husband. And I so happen to be your lawyer. You'll have to leave it up to me."

"I didn't hire you as my lawyer, Chase."

"I bailed you out so, technically, I am."

My thoughts were racing, and at last I took a deep breath. "I get it. What Clint does is terrible and I agree that he needs to be punished. But why don't you just move on and let karma do its job? Why is it so important to you to get even with Clint? I'm not saying I'm justifying what he does; I'm just trying to understand why you're still living in the past when you and your brother are clearly doing well. I mean, Kade owns LiveInvent. Talk about wow. That's a huge accomplishment. And you don't seem poor, either."

It was true.

LiveInvent was where the big-shot strategists and best marketing professionals worked. In the few years it had operated, it had quickly become a household name among celebrities and famous brands, and my big dream ever since

172

I realized they were behind almost every major campaign that had won a prize in the past years.

"It took us ten years to build LiveInvent. It didn't happen overnight," Chase said. "But you're right. There's a reason why it's so important for me to get revenge."

I held my breath as I realized the moment I had been waiting for had come.

"Clint is the reason my father committed suicide," Chase said. "When my dad couldn't repay Clint's loan, we weren't just miles in debt; we ended up homeless and without any hope. My father was desperate, not because he had just lost his business. My mom grew sick, very sick, and there were medical bills we couldn't pay. When the medical insurance company refused to pay, my father drove of a cliff." His voice broke.

"You said your parents died in a road accident when you were nine," I said.

He shook his head. "It was a lie, Laurie. I couldn't tell you the truth, not when we barely knew each other."

"I'm sorry." I looked up and flinched at the intensity in his eyes filled with pain.

"There's nothing you can do," Chase said. "There's nothing anyone could have done. For a long time, we thought it had been an accident, until we found the note. He had killed himself out of desperation, so that we'd get his life insurance money to pay for my mom's medical treatment. He did it so that my brother and I could still go to college and have a future; so that my mom would get well. Needless to say, my mom's treatment came too late and she didn't make it." His gaze pierced my heart, his gray blue eyes both beautiful and shattering. "So, as you can see, we have more in common than you think," he whispered. "We've both lost our parents thanks to Clint."

I let out a shaky breath. Chase's words felt raw, intimate. In fact, they were more intimate than anything he had ever told me.

"I'm sorry," I whispered. "I had no idea."

I wanted to reach out to him, to comfort him, take away the pain, while another part of me demanded that I stay away.

He shrugged, as though his life story wasn't a big deal. "It's fine." He looked away. "Now you know why I have to do it. My father was a victim. We all were. Believe it or not, I do care about you," he said quietly. "But this is something I owe my family. Because everything he owns is connected to your inheritance, I can make him suffer. For once, I want him to feel the pain we felt. I want him to lose something he loves—and in his case that's money."

"That's why you married me," I said to process the news. Shaking my head, I poured myself another glass of wine and gulped it all down. Only after the liquid had traveled down my throat, leaving a bitter trail in its wake, did I turn to face Chase.

"You wasted your time," I said softly. "Even if I wanted to help, all I get is a quarter. If you had been upfront with me before, I would have been able to help you. You shouldn't have lied and tricked me into believing you cared for me. I would have understood. But now the whole thing was in vain. I signed an agreement before I married you, so the inheritance is practically his."

"Is it?" Chase counteracted.

"Is what?" I asked, confused.

"Is the inheritance still his if he never received the signed agreement?"

My eyes narrowed as I took in his words. Was it my imagination or had his expression softened?

"What do you mean?" I asked. "I gave him the signed agreement before we got married."

"That may be true, but what if the contract you signed disappeared?" He leaned forward conspiratorially. "Maybe it never existed. Would you say it was still valid?"

I shook my head, confused.

"Of course it exists. I signed it." I stared at him. "What are you getting at? It sounds as though you're trying to pull me into that gray legal area with you, and I'm not interested in getting involved."

He leaned back against the seat. "I might or might not have it."

175

My heart skipped a beat. Then another. I felt as though I was stuck on a roller coaster ride and everything was going too fast.

"You do not have it," I said slowly. "Because if you did—"

It would be illegal—just like about everything else that involved Chase.

"Okay, maybe I don't have it, but I did until it burned."

"You broke into Clint's home and stole the contract?" I asked in disbelief.

He regarded me with an amused glint in his eyes. "Not into his home, but his lawyer's."

I let out a brief laugh.

Holy shit.

The guy was trouble.

"That breaks the law on so many levels." I shook my head, unable to comprehend the way his mind worked. "Chase, you're a lawyer. At least that's what you're claiming to be. Why would you do that? Aren't you supposed to stick to the rules?"

He cocked a brow. "Do I look like a cop? No, I'm a lawyer, and in all the years I worked as one, I learned a lot. Sometimes, to achieve a goal, you have to break the rules," he said. "Everyone does it because the law's corrupt. Ask any lawyer and he'll tell you the same thing. Clint doesn't have the right to take what's yours. He had no right to take what was *ours*. Now that I'm your husband, I have the power and the right to take legal action against him."

"Was that really your plan all along?"

"To contest your mom's will? Yes." He nodded his head, the motion strengthening his words.

"Even if I wanted to, I can't allow it," I said frightened at the thought of welcoming more chaos into my life.

"When I said you won't have a choice, I meant it, Laurie," he said. "You should have asked for a prenup. Without one, I have access to everything that belongs to you, unless you get a divorce, in which case you won't see your mom's letters."

Maybe what he said was true, and maybe it wasn't.

For the first time, I realized how naïve I had been. He was a lawyer, I wasn't. He was prepared to do whatever it took to further his agenda; I wasn't.

I swallowed hard, but couldn't quite get rid of the lump lodged in my throat.

"It's not your right to interfere in my life," I said angrily. "Just so you know, Clint never forced me to give him anything. I did it freely. He's been offering me money for years—money I never took."

"I know that." Chase nodded slowly. "Your mom told you not to take anything, right? It's the reason you gave up everything."

My whole body tensed.

He was right.

It was the *only* reason, something I might have mentioned to him. But he knew way more than the bits and pieces of information I had fed him.

"Don't ever talk about my mom again. It was her wish that Clint receive the money, so I'm going to respect it."

"Laurie," he started, his voice serious, heavy. "Did you ever stop to think about *why* she would demand something like that from her daughter? Your own mother out of all people." He inched closer to me until his thigh brushed mine. I peered at it for a second, unsure whether to put some distance between us, when he resumed the conversation. "Did it never occur to you that maybe she was forced? That maybe she had no choice? That maybe she was fearing for her life?"

Slowly, his face came closer, his hot breath brushing my lips. "Think, Laurie. The entire estate belonged to your mom. It's been in your family for generations—not just money, but heirlooms. You really think anyone would give it away to someone they've known for a few years rather than their own child?"

"I'm sure she had her reasons," I protested weakly, even though I knew he was right.

The same thoughts had occurred to me years ago. They had kept circling in my mind, coming and going at regular intervals. Even Jude had tried to pinpoint it to me, and I had brushed her off simply because I could feel just how right she was.

"And yet Clint insists that you get a fraction of your inheritance," Chase said coolly. "Do you know why he wants you to have it? As your lawyer, I can tell you it's so you won't be able to contest the terms of the will later, once you find out your mom wasn't well. That's why he wanted a written agreement. If you simply refused to sign, you would have received everything. And then there's another matter."

"What?" I asked faintly.

"Your grandparents were the actual owners of Waterfront Shore. Your mom was their heir, followed by you. Your grandfather was still alive when she died, which is why I think Clint adopted you. She was living there, yes, but the entire estate never belonged to your mom in the first place. By adopting you Clint became your legal guardian, meaning he got the estate through you once your grandfather passed away. Legally speaking, her testament should never have been implemented because the estate had never been passed on to her. I think she left that legal loophole open because she knew something was off about Clint."

I leaned back, both in shock and realization, my thoughts racing. "Are you saying my mom wanted me to have the inheritance?" My voice dripped with disbelief.

"Yes."

I shook my head. "I don't believe you."

"Well, that's too bad." I frowned at his words. "I have every reason to believe that your mom's letters contain her real thoughts on the matter."

His words made my head spin. "How do you know all this?"

He smiled gently. "The law is complex, particularly when you're a minor and your legal guardian, the one person who should be looking out for you, has only his own gain in mind. I don't believe your mom was as crazy as Clint made her out to be. I believe she was scared. In fact, so scared that she put it in writing."

He hadn't answered my question.

I shook my head again. My hands were clammy and trembling. The past I had left behind was catching up with me. I needed to be alone, if only to figure out my next step.

"The ten minutes are over, Chase," I said weakly. "Tell the driver to stop the car."

"We'll reach the hotel in a few minutes."

"I want to leave now!"

Chase grimaced. "Laurie, you don't even know where you are."

"That's not your problem," I said harsher than intended. "Stop the car, Chase."

He sighed, and then he pressed a button. "As you wish."

Within seconds, the limousine came to a halt. As soon

as the door opened, I jumped out and took off down the street without a glance back.

Chapter 15

THE STREETS WERE cramped, so avoiding people wasn't easy. I walked down the busy road with no idea where I was. A few taxis drove by. I ignored them all. The hotel couldn't be far away, but I didn't feel like locking myself up. I needed the walk to process Chase's words. Everything inside my mind was a blur, but if I concentrated hard enough, I could hear my mom's voice.

It had been on one of those days where she was lucid enough to talk and remember she still had a daughter. She'd brought me to my bed, a soft smile on her pale lips.

"You can never trust a man, baby girl," my mom whispered. "Don't make the same mistake I did. Don't fall in love. Don't trust them, because all men are the same.

They betray you, hurt you, and take away your innocence."

I glanced at her, assured I would always listen to her, the way I always did, and told her I would always love her—my words those of a child, trusting, truthful, unconditional.

At that time, I was only seven and had no clue about the world or love. She pressed me real hard against her chest, telling me how much she loved me and how often she had thought of running away with me to keep me safe; that she couldn't deal with another loss.

Back then, I had no idea what she meant.

But now I wished I had listened; I wished I remembered more, if only to get a glimpse into the workings of her mind; to see her beautiful face once more, hear her voice, feel the soft touch of her hand on my cheek.

A stray tear trickled down my face as I forced my legs to keep moving through the busy streets of Acapulco. Inside me, chaos, pain, and more chaos roared, the remembrances of my mother and her immediate loss too heavy to bear.

I missed her. Missed her smell, her smile, her hugs.

In my memories, she was always pale, her face framed by beautiful dark curls, and her warm brown eyes always smiling. Her fingers were long and thin—a pianist's hands as some would say—and she always smelled clean with a hint of lavender.

Conjuring her picture before my eyes made me think of how unlucky she was to die so young, how depressed she

183

must have been to jump off the cliff. Or maybe it wasn't depression but desperation that drove her to commit suicide, just like Chase's dad drove off a cliff because he couldn't provide for his family.

When Chase mentioned that my mom had been scared for her life, I knew that he was right. After all, my mother had locked me inside my bedroom on a regular basis and sent me away to boarding schools, as if the Waterfront Shore wasn't safe. As if she couldn't risk having me around.

As a child, I had always assumed her fear was all in her head.

But now?

I wasn't sure of anything anymore.

Had Clint hurt her?

The possibility of him hurting her scared me. Still, as much as I wanted to, I just couldn't image him being a violent man.

Sneaky and manipulative, yes.

But violent?

He was obsessive compulsive to the point of disliking to touch things and people. When I grew up, he had made it pretty clear that any physical proximity was out of the question. The only real hug he ever gave me was at my mom's funeral and a few weeks ago, during his first visit in years.

Ahead was a market, the smell of food pungent.

Hastening my steps, I tried not to inhale too deeply out of fear that my nausea would return with a vengeance. I passed the market and the rough buildings to either side. I was so engrossed in my past that I only heard the steps behind me when they were within arm's reach. I turned quickly, almost expecting Chase.

But it wasn't him.

A guy in his twenties, dressed in a blue shirt and jeans, looked down at me.

My heart lurched in my chest.

I stopped to rummage through my bag to grab my phone, ready to speed-dial someone while I stared straight at his face. I'd read somewhere that if you ever found yourself followed, the best way to handle the situation was to get a good look at your pursuer to signal them that you'd remember their face, and aren't easy prey.

To my relief, the guy barely looked at me as he walked past, then turned a corner. My glance followed him as he disappeared around the corner.

I let out a long breath and leaned against the wall, my phone pressed tightly against my chest. My breathing slowed down a little, but my heart didn't stop hammering.

Why the fuck did I think it was Chase? As if he'd follow after me when I had made myself clear that I wanted nothing to do with him.

"Stupid," I muttered and pushed the phone back into

my bag. A glance at my watch showed that I had been walking for an hour.

Where was the frigging hotel?

That's when I noticed the crowd of five guys heading in my direction. Worse yet, I caught their curious glances, two of them even checking me out. Someone made a remark, and they all laughed.

My heart started to pick up in speed again, and my entire body tensed.

Should I keep on walking or turn around?

I had no idea.

One of them shouted, "Hola bonita."

I froze to the spot, and my uneasiness turned into panic. Before I could decide what to do, a hand touched my waist, and I jumped, a scream lodged in my throat.

I turned and stared right into Chase's face.

His expression was one of worry, his posture tense. I knew I should be mad, and yet I couldn't bring myself to do anything but shoot him a hesitant smile as immense relief washed over me.

He bent forward and for a moment I thought he was going to kiss me, until his lips brushed my ear.

"Keep on walking," he whispered. His grip around my waist tightened just a little bit, but there was nothing sexual about the gesture.

His tension was palpable.

I nodded and resumed my walk, keeping my head low.

The moment we past the crowd I turned to him and hissed, "Are you following me?"

"Only to ensure your safety." He didn't even try to deny it.

"Why do you care?" I asked.

"Believe it or not, I don't want you to get hurt. And you're walking in the wrong direction." He pointed behind him. "The hotel's that way."

Of course I had been walking in the wrong direction. I groaned inwardly. I should have called a taxi a long time ago.

"Where's your driver?" I asked and peered around me even though there was no sight of the limousine.

"I sent him home. Do you want me to call him?"

The thought of spending more time in a confined space made my heart race—and not exactly in a bad way.

Judging from the slow smirk on his face he knew it.

Why the fuck did I have to ask?

"No. Forget it." I shielded my eyes against the hot sun and turned away from him.

"Let me take you home, Laurie," Chase said softly, misinterpreting my words. "As soon as you're inside the lobby, I'll leave you alone. I promise."

I sighed. "It's not that." I turned back to regard him. "I'm actually glad you're here."

He frowned. "You are?"

"Believe it or not, I am," I said, echoing his expression from earlier. It was true. I was in a foreign country with absolutely no knowledge of the culture and barely any command of the language.

"Doesn't mean I forgive you, though. What you did is—"

"Despicable. I know. And I couldn't agree more."

"But I'm really glad you're here. I kind of felt followed. And—" I wriggled my hands, suddenly unsure why I was telling him all that.

"By me?" he asked.

"No, by a guy in a blue shirt."

We reached the market—people spilling in and out, chatting, carrying bags. I had never seen such a commotion in my entire life. I wasn't scared of crowds, but my nerves were frayed.

"Have you been inside?" he asked, pointing toward the market.

I cocked my head, regarding him amused. "Well, you tell me. You followed me for a good hour."

"Did I?" Chase asked. I looked up, surprised at his question. "I'm afraid I didn't notice. I was too transfixed."

And there it was again.

The humor in his voice.

The sparkle in his eyes.

To my absolute disbelief, my heart started to flutter again.

"On what?" My eyes narrowed.

"Want me to be honest?" His eyes moved down my body and lingered on my ass a bit too long.

My body temperature rose a few degrees and my breathing came labored.

He had been transfixed by my *ass*?

Oh, God.

"No," I mumbled. "Don't say it."

"In a marriage you shouldn't have to be hiding things."

I squealed as he slapped my ass lightly.

"Come on," Chase said, "I'd kill for an ice cream. Do you think they sell it inside?"

I glanced at the market and the commotion of people flooding in and out. "Let's find out."

Back in California, I had often visited markets simply because I loved the atmosphere. This one was the best I had ever seen. It wasn't just huge, colorful and bubbly, there was so much to see I didn't know where to look first. My gaze jumped from the gorgeous flower bouquets, to the homemade food, to the handmade pottery, and everything else.

I stopped a stall that sold shirts for only a few pesos. One read, 'Be calm and let Acapulco handle it.'

"I should get one for Jude," I said to Chase, my voice

dripping with excitement, then pointed to a range of key rings. "And one of those, too."

He shrugged, seemingly bored by it all. Yeah, guys and shopping. I laughed, elated at the thought that I was *here* with *him*.

"I'll try to find us some ice cream while you have a look."

Before he could disappear through the crowd, I called after him. "Chase?"

He turned around, the light reflecting in his eyes in a million facets of blue and gray. "Yeah?"

"Just so we're clear, this is not a date."

"I got the memo, and discarded it just as quickly." He grinned and then he winked.

I laughed.

Oh, my God. He was the devil.

And then he disappeared, leaving me to check out everything. My credit cards were maxed out, but I figured, so what?

You didn't go to Acapulco and came back with nothing?

Almost giggling with excitement, I bought three shirts: one for Jude, and two for me because they were a bargain. And then I decided that I had to get one for Chase, too.

Flicking through the clothes hangers, I settled on one that read 'Walking Danger' which sort of described him down to a T.

It was so perfect for him, I couldn't wait to show it to him.

I let out a giggle as I paid for it, then grabbed my shopping bags and headed through the crowd in search for Chase.

I found him standing in line in front of a stall. I had almost reached him when someone blocked my way. It was the same guy who had followed me. Maybe he hadn't followed me per se, but I had spotted him on the street outside. Up close, he didn't look older than eighteen.

He spoke so fast I couldn't follow.

I smiled apologetically. "Sorry. No hablo espanol."

"No hay problema." He returned the smile, then opened his bag, and my heart stopped as I peered inside at the various bags of weed, pills and other drugs.

Holy shit.

He was a drug dealer.

"No, thank you." I shook my head, making sure to smile politely. But somehow, he didn't seem to understand. Instead leaving, he reached inside and retrieved a tiny plastic bag containing a single pill.

"Regalo." He stretched out his hand.

Oh, god.

I shook my head more resolutely. "No, thank you."

The guy grabbed my hand and squeezed the bag inside my palm, muttering a few more words in Spanish. I shook my head. Before I could protest, I glimpsed over his shoulder and caught Chase storming for us, his face a mask of anger.

My entire body tensed.

I tried to step back, but it was too late.

Chase shoved him. "Get the fuck away from her." And then he did the unthinkable: he shoved him again, this time way harder, before I could tell him to stop.

The guy's friendliness was wiped off his face instantly. I stared helplessly as Chase turned to me, asking, "Are you okay, Laurie? Was he bothering you?"

Before I could react, the guy's fist connected with Chase's jaw, the impact so hard I could have sworn I heard bones cracking.

Chase's body lurched forward, his hands going to his lip as blood started to pour between his fingers and drip down his chin. I rushed forward just as the guy took off through the crowd.

"Oh, god. Chase." I dropped my bags and began to rummage through my handbag in search for a tissue.

"I know I shouldn't have interfered," he muttered and wiped a hand over his mouth.

Horrified, I peered at the red stains on his shirt.

"No, you shouldn't have. It was plain stupid. You're lucky the guy didn't pull out a gun."

While Chase pressed the tissue against his mouth to stop

the bleeding, I quickly scrolled through my contact list to find the most recent number I had saved: Kade.

"What are you doing?" Chase asked warily.

"I'm calling your brother."

He placed his hand on the screen, blocking my view. "Don't."

The command came forceful.

I frowned. "Why not? You're bleeding." I stared at his split lip and winced. The bit of pressure did nothing to stop the blood flow. "Quite heavily, I might add, and you clearly need medical assistance Besides, I can't drag you all the way to the hotel all by myself."

"It's nothing." He swatted his hand, as though we were talking about an annoying fly. "It doesn't even hurt."

I stared at him, having my doubts. His upper lip, now swollen, looked horrific. His nose didn't look swollen, but there was blood. I hoped it wasn't broken. "We should get you a mirror, because in all honesty, it looks like you need stitches."

"What is it with you women and your tendency to exaggerate? The next thing you'll be doing is dragging met to a nearby hospital."

"I was going to suggest that," I said dryly.

He laughed until he noticed my expression. "This—" He pointed to the split lip "—is nothing. My brother and I fought a lot, so I'm pretty used to a little bit of blood and a bruise or two. Frankly, if we're being absolutely honest, I let that kid beat me on purpose to get your attention."

I crossed my arms over my chest and regarded him in mock disbelief. "Yeah, right. That's what *you* say."

"Trust me when I say I could have easily beaten his ass." He grinned, swollen lip and all, and I couldn't help but shake my head, marveling at his ego. "The fact that you're still here makes me think you're the kind of woman who's into tough guys. Since you seem more into boxers than lawyers, I could change my profession for you," Chase said. "For you, I'd do anything."

"Great," I muttered. "Now you're delirious, too. Your head must have been hit."

He chuckled and fished his phone out of his pocket. "I'm calling the driver to pick us up. We're having ice cream."

I stared at him. "You're kidding, right?"

"I don't see why we shouldn't."

I shook my head. "Chase, you can't run around like this. Tell your driver to pick you up and take you back to your hotel." I bit my lip, my thoughts a hailstorm as I watched Chase busy himself with his phone.

"Where are you staying, by the way?" I asked as soon as he had finished the call.

"Why are you asking? Are you thinking of paying me a visit?" His eyebrows rose.

"No, Chase." Emphasis on 'no'. "I'm definitely not sleeping with you again, if that's what you're thinking about."

"Who said anything about sex? See, you're the one with the dirty mind." He smirked and I rolled my eyes. "You just keep mentioning it. It's like you can't think of anything else when you're around me."

His ego was unbelievable.

"What?"

"I was thinking of my mouth needing some—" he babbled something undistinguishable, then pointed to his lip. "Sorry, it's really hard to speak. On a second thought, it really hurts. Maybe you could help a man out here."

I inched closer and touched his cheek before I realized it was all a pretense so I'd feel sorry for him.

It was working. But it wasn't that I felt sorry for him. He hadn't been completely wrong about the tough guys part.

"You'd better not be trying what I think you're trying right now," I said. "You're not exactly sexy with all that blood on your face." I scowled which only had him laughing out loud. "Just to be clear, the only reason I'd accompany you to your hotel is to make sure you don't end up jumped on by someone else."

His laugh bellowed behind me as we left the marketplace and returned back to the street. Waiting for the limousine, I turned to Chase. "Where are you staying? You never told me."

His lips twitched. "I'm afraid to disclose that bit of information, but only almost."

"Almost? Why would you…" I broke off mid-sentence and stared at him.

Why the hell was he smiling? And why the hell did his eyes shimmer like he was up to no good?

Slowly, realization kicked in.

No way.

I closed my eyes and gave an exasperated sigh. "Please don't tell me you're camped at the same hotel, Chase."

Because that was exactly the kind of thing I should have expected from Chase.

"I am," he said with a smug grin. "The place isn't so bad. However, I do have some concerns. The walls are so thin I swear I'll be able to hear you take a shower and that'll drive me crazy if I can't join you. And why didn't you choose a hotel that offers certain bedroom services or adult channels?"

I narrowed my eyes on him. "What for? So you can watch porn?"

"I thought you weren't jealous."

"I'm not." I groaned inwardly as heat traveled up my chest and settled in my face. "Like you were saying, the walls are too thin. No one needs to hear your private business while you're watching that stuff."

"I thought you might be into watching it together."

Hell, no.

The only naked booty I wanted Chase to see was mine.

Jealous?

Hell, yeah. I was.

My cheeks flamed up even more.

"Your face says it all. As long as we're married, I won't look at any other woman" Chase said, as though reading my thoughts, and inched just a little bit closer. "I can be a patient man, Laurie, though I don't think I'll have to wait particularly long until you're back in my bed. But to ease your worries, and to be absolutely clear, you do not owe me."

I stared at him, my blood boiling.

Those were the exact words I had told Jude.

"I think I'm going to kill you." I muttered. "You did not book yourself into the same hotel. Please tell me you didn't."

"Why would you make such a statement when you know you're wrong." He winked. "In fact, I went to all the trouble to book the room next to yours. I thought it'd save us time."

"Save us time in what way?"

"The time you waste between getting that booty call and arriving at the designated meeting place. The quicker you're there, the faster you can get to the fun part." He laughed out loud, seemingly pleased with his reasoning.

I stared at him, open-mouthed.

His sexy smile curved into a panty-dropping grin. My heartbeat went through the roof.

He was right, of course. If I were to want to pay him a visit in the middle of the night, the location of his room mattered a great deal. However, as much as the idea appealed to me, it wasn't going to happen.

"Is your brother staying with you?" I turned away from him, changing the subject.

"Of course not." He sighed. I could feel his gaze on me. "What? You still don't believe me that I had no idea he was here?"

I rolled my eyes. "No, I don't. You're a liar."

"Only when I have no other choice. Unfortunately, your trust issues are beginning to turn into a problem. I'll sign us up for therapy as soon as we're back home."

What?

"What do we need a therapy for?" I asked.

"We need to build trust if we want to save this relationship."

This relationship.

"We don't have a relationship, Chase." Hopefully, if I said it often enough, my stupid heart would stop skipping beats at every single meaningless word of his.

"On paper, we do." He grinned. "I'm still your husband,

aren't I? That should count for something."

"Fake husband," I stated the obvious.

"No one would agree with you now that we've consummated the marriage." He was smiling, but his tone was serious. I sensed we were entering that gray legal area of his again.

"It was a mistake," I mumbled.

"I don't think that's the way you feel." His eyebrows shot up. "I think, given the chance, you'd repeat the experience in a heartbeat. You know how I know?"

I knew I should take the bait and yet I couldn't help myself. "How?"

"You're wet. A man has his ways of telling."

"You're unbelievable and the kind of jerk my mother would have warned me about." I stared at him as the limo pulled up next to us, his laughter strangely intoxicating. Heat settled between my legs. I pressed them together, realizing that I was wet. Very much so.

"Maybe," Chase whispered. "But I actually think she would have given you her blessing."

Chapter 16

THROUGHOUT THE DRIVE back to the hotel, my
mind kept wandering back to his words about my mom and
the way he had looked when he spoke them. However, as
much as I would have liked to talk about it, we had more
pressing issues to attend to.

Such as his split lip and the fact that he had just taken a
beating for me.

"Why didn't you tell your brother that we got married?"
I asked back at the hotel.

Chase was sitting on my bed. I was kneeling at his feet,
wiping caked blood off his lips. Every touch sent my heart
racing. Strangely, in spite of the intimacy, the gesture felt
natural—as if I had always done little things for him.

His lip was still swollen, but at least he was clean.

"I thought you guys were close," I added, my gaze focused on his beautiful face.

"We are," he said. "That's the thing. He's my best friend."

"Didn't look that way when you two met in the hall."

"That's because we got in a fight before you and I married." The way he said it made me stop and listen up.

"About what?" I put away the wet towel and sat down on the bed, eyeing him in the silence of the room. He looked exhausted, but more than that, he had a wild glint in his eyes that didn't escape me.

It must have been a taxing fight.

"About you," he mumbled.

"Hmm."

The heaviness of the situation was oppressing. Unsure what to do with myself, I decided that I needed to keep both my hands and my mind busy—anything, just not look at him.

Resuming my position, I dived the towel into the bowl of alcohol and wrung it, then pressed it back against his wound.

"Why?" My voice came low, strangled.

His eyes remained glued to me for a few seconds. At last, he sighed. "I don't know."

I frowned. "You don't know?"

"Okay, I know why we fought. I don't get why he acted the way he did. It's like he doesn't get it."

"Get what?"

His fingers circled around mine, and he pulled me onto his lap, his body close, his scent irresistible. "Would you believe me if I told you that I'm starting to fall in love with you?"

My breath died in my throat. My vision swam. My knees grew weak. His honesty surprised me, shocked me, confused me.

My words remained lodged inside my brain.

"You..." I shook my head, frowning. "Why?"

"Why? Really? You're asking me the same thing he did?" He groaned. "I told him that I had feelings for you. His response was that it's impossible to fall in love with someone so quickly and that I shouldn't let my feelings interfere with our plan." His grip on my fingers tightened, as though unconsciously he was trying to hold on to me. "He was afraid I wouldn't go through with the wedding to get the inheritance."

"But you did," I said.

"Yeah, but..." He looked up. His eyes met mine in something deep and intimate. "I also did it because I like you. And because I cannot bear you dating anyone else but me. Particularly not my brother."

"I don't know why you keep saying that. He isn't even

my type." I blurted out the words before I could stop to think what I was saying.

"He isn't?" Chase asked, his gloomy expression slowly lifting.

I shook my head. "No."

"Then who is?"

I looked away, but not before a smile tugged at my lips.

We both knew it. No point in denying it. But I didn't want to spell out the obvious either.

"Then why would you want to go out with someone other than me?" he asked.

My attention turned back to him, my breath coming out shallow. "Maybe because I was trying hard to move on from you."

"Do you still want to, now that you know the truth?"

I swallowed.

Did I?

"Probably, yes," I whispered. Was it the truth? I didn't know. "But it doesn't mean I haven't developed feelings for you, too."

His hand moved to the nape of my neck. Slowly, he leaned forward and his lips met mine.

Closing my eyes, I surrendered to his kiss.

He kissed me as if I was a delicate flower.

As if time had stopped.

As if he and I were the only people in the world.

His lips parted gently, silently urging me to deepen the kiss. And I did so willingly, letting his tongue explore my mouth.

I lay down on the bed, and his body moved between my parted legs. His hands began to roam over my body, trailing up the naked skin of my thighs as he pulled up my dress.

I stopped his hand, but only for a second. "Chase?"

"Hmm?" His eyes were hooded, mirroring my own lust.

"This will be the last time," I whispered and arched my back, signaling that I was more than ready for him.

Chapter 17

FOR A MOMENT, Chase stared at me, his eyes shimmering with desire intermingled with countless unspoken questions, as though he couldn't believe my invitation. And then he began to undress me in a hurry, his hands flying over my body, squeezing beneath my clothes.

His lips started to kiss my naked skin, leaving a wet trail behind. I let him touch me, caught up in the heat of the moment, and moaned as his hand moved in determined strokes over my inner thighs.

"You're really something," Chase whispered.

"I hope that's a good thing."

"The best."

My body yearned for his touch, my mind marveling at

the heat his hands left behind. Cupping my breasts, he sucked one nipple in between his lips, then paid the same attention to the other, until they became so hard it almost hurt.

I threw my head back and pulled him on top of me, my body shivered against burning skin. My fingers roamed over his back, his broad shoulders, and finally settled in his silky hair. I wanted him naked. I wanted him inside me, filling me, stretching me.

"You sure kept me waiting," Chase murmured and pried my legs apart, settling between my thighs. His breath brushed my naked skin, my most sensitive spot.

"All good things are worth the wait," I said.

Especially you.

"You're so right about that."

As soon as his tongue licked my clit, I moved.

"Don't," I whispered.

My words stopped him. With clouded eyes, he gazed at me. "Why not?"

"I won't be able to control myself."

"I have all time in the world, if that's what worries you."

I shook my head. "I don't want to wait. I need you now," I whispered.

"You sure?" As if to point out what I'd be missing, his tongue brushed my clit again, and again, his fingers rubbing against my folds, almost sending me over the edge.

"Very sure," I half-whispered, half-moaned, and let out a sudden gasp as his tongue probed my entry.

Oh, my God.

It felt so good.

My sex clenched, fueled by the soft, penetrating motion of his tongue.

"Fuck me, Chase," I whispered. "Fuck me, now."

His fingers pulled back.

The sudden emptiness surprised me.

Had he listened to my command?

I opened my eyes and saw him standing. The look in his eyes was fierce and wild.

"What are you doing?" I mumbled.

Why the fuck wasn't he moving?

Undressing?

Doing *something,* rather than just staring at my exposed flesh?

I lifted one leg high up in the air to give him all the view he wanted. It was something I never thought I'd be doing for a man—be proactive, straightforward with my desire.

"If it's going to be the last time, then I'll do it on my own terms," Chase said, his eyes hooded. "I want you to do as I say when I say it."

I nodded, fascinated by his pure primal energy. He peeled off his shirt and jeans. My tongue wet my suddenly dry lips as he removed his belt and unbuttoned his jeans to reveal his magnificent erection.

I expected him to drop the belt. Instead, he held it up. "I'll hold on to this."

He leapt onto the bed.

My heartbeat quickened as his hand grabbed my wrists, pinning me to the spot. The belt went around my wrists and the headboard, his touch gentle but definite, the look in his eyes, something I had never seen before.

It was dominant, and possessive. And so fucking sexy. His voice was husky, his breath hot against my suddenly cold skin.

"You're not going to forget me," he whispered in my ear.

As if anyone would.

His voice was deep and strained, filled with control and so much desire, I knew it could easily match mine.

My body trembled as I watched him kneel and take his hard cock into his hand, his fingers moving up and down his hard shaft, his eyes never leaving me. The strokes were slow and measured, his breathing raspy, as his gaze traced every inch of me, lingering on my breasts, the soft spot between my legs.

His heady smell permeated the air, making me painfully aware just how much I wanted him. My sex clenched again, my mouth watered at the thought teasing him the way I knew he was about to tease me.

"Let me taste you," I begged, eager to take him into my mouth.

"Not today, baby. Today it's all about you."

I couldn't stop the shudder running through me as he moved between my legs, spreading them wide apart to settle between my thighs. Two fingers squeezed inside me, probing, stretching. I moaned and lifted my hips just a little bit, urging him to go deeper.

"You're wet for me," Chase growled, his tone almost feral.

How could I tell him that I was always wet for him? Always ready.

"Tell me what you want, Laurie." The command was sharp. Not answering was not an option.

"I want you to fuck me," I whispered, my eyes locked with his. "Just tonight. For the last time."

His eyes darkened, but not with lust. Flames of anger flashed through them, turning the gray blue a few shades darker.

"As you wish."

His hands busied themselves with the belt, tightening even though I could barely move my wrists.

I closed my eyes, feeling him settling, the head of his cock against my folds, my wetness coating him a moment before he slid inside me, one inch at a time. I felt my mind losing focus. Another shudder rocked me as he thrust into me until I could take no more and shifted, the size and weight of his cock too big.

A bit uncomfortable, too tight.

And yet the burning and desire didn't stop.

I wanted more.

I wanted everything he had to give.

His hand moved down to my clit, rubbing it in slow, relentless strokes, until the pressure inside me built up, ready to throw me over the edge.

"Don't fight it, Laurie." His voice was hoarse, aroused by the fact that he was deep inside me twitching, but not moving, stretching me, but not giving me the friction I so desperately sought.

We were connected, linked, my body shaking with exhaustion, screaming for the release only he could give me.

Soon, I knew, I would come, no matter whether he moved or not, because his fingers were doing a hell of a job.

The oncoming climax was hanging over my head like a sword.

"Please just fuck me," I begged.

"Not yet. You're too tight for me. I want you to be completely wet, otherwise it's going to hurt." His tone was strained, as though he was having a hard time controlling himself.

His words made no sense.

I was wet, wasn't I?

His fingers moved faster while his body and his cock stood still. My hips lifted to grant him deeper access.

He groaned but didn't move.

Damn it.

His fingers moved faster. The pulsating ache between my legs intensified. And then I felt it. My body relaxed, and my insides began to burn. A moan escaped my breath as his fingers continued to rub the sensitive spot one more time before he pulled out and then plunged his cock deep inside me, spreading me wide open.

My pulse spiked. I opened my eyes and caught his intense gaze.

"Please," I whispered, ready to beg some more.

"By the time I'm done, I'm going to be so deep inside you, you'll never think of another man again."

Please, as if anyone could ever take his place inside my mind. Or heart. Or pussy.

I shook my head, my eyes wild. The pressure was too much, the waves of lust and pleasure rocking me too hard. I flicked my tongue over my parched lips.

"Chase." His name found its way past my lips as I peered down at the spot where our bodies connected.

He pulled out almost to his crown, the moisture glittering on his long shaft. And then he leaned forward and kissed me hard, his mouth crushing mine just as his cock thrust inside me in one straight move.

All the way in.

He had never kissed me so wildly before. His cock had never been so deep inside me.

His mouth stifled my moans while his fingers resumed their torture on my clit.

Slowly at first, he began to move, his thrusts measured while his lips moved to my neck, my collarbone, my cheeks, and then back to my lips. My body tightened, my chest heaved as I started to rock against him to meet his hips.

"Lift your legs higher," he commanded.

The air cold against my feverish skin, I obeyed and fully opened myself to his thrusts. His movements became harder and faster, as if he wanted to bury himself deep into me. My vision began to spin, and the initial pulses changed to tremors. My hands struggled against their restrains. Closing my eyes, I moved my hips against his, but it was impossible to keep up his speed.

"Chase," I cried a moment before every muscle in my body tensed.

And then the climax crashed through me.

It didn't take long for him to follow. One more hit, and the second orgasm rocked through me.

Fucking hell.

I smiled, savoring the moment because I knew our moment together wouldn't last.

Chapter 18

THE PHONE KEPT ringing, the annoying sound echoing in my brain. I pulled the pillow over my head, debating whether to throw the phone against the wall or give up hope on any sleep and pick up.

It had to be Jude, I just knew it. Everyone else wouldn't be so persistent.

I stretched out my hand from under the covers and grabbed it, keeping my eyes closed as I responded. "Yeah?"

"Laurie." Jude's frantic voice echoed at the other end. "You promised to call."

I winced at her shrill tone and pressed my eyes tightly shut. The pounding in my head was merciless and hard—as if a sledgehammer was working hard to split my skull open.

"Please stop shouting. I'm so tired I can barely keep my eyes open."

Which was true. I barely got any sleep last night.

"Sorry. I wouldn't have called if it wasn't important."

I sighed and tossed the pillow aside. "All right. What's going on?"

"Clint called."

The two words were enough to freeze my blood in my veins.

I rose instantly, all sleep gone, and blinked against the glaring morning sun flooding in through the window. A glance at the bedside clock told me it was ten a.m. so it had to be late morning in NYC, where Jude was staying, and early morning in California, where Clint lived.

The sun spilled its unnerving rays into the bedroom, lighting it up like a shrine. I got up and pulled the curtains, the semi-darkness providing instant relief.

"Did you hear what I just said?" Jude asked. "I just got off the phone with Clint."

"What did he want?" I asked with a sense of dread in the pit of my stomach.

"He wants to know where you are, but don't worry, I didn't blab," Jude said.

"Did he say why he wants to know where I am?"

"Yes, he did." She paused, hesitating. "He asked why you went to court behind his back. He said you and he had a deal, and that you broke it." She sounded concerned. "Are you taking him to court, Laurie? He sounded real mad and threatened you with consequences."

Oh, shit.

All the blood rushed out of my face as my hands started to sweat. Letting myself fall on my back, I closed my eyes and willed myself to take deep breaths.

They didn't calm me down one bit.

Worse yet, panic rose inside me as my mind recalled Chase's words, his plans, his intentions.

He was moving forward with his plans.

It was all his fault.

I didn't have to consider the possibility, I just knew. After all, he had warned me of what he was about to do, but for some stupid reason, I thought after last night he'd change his mind; that I had more time, that he'd respect my wishes.

I had been wrong *again*.

"What's going on?" Jude probed carefully, drawing my attention back to her. "I'm sure this is some kind of misunderstanding. I mean, obviously you didn't take legal actions against your stepfather. He must be crazy to think you'd do that." She let out a nervous laugh. "Or would you?"

"No, I wouldn't." I shook my head and began to massage my temples.

"See, I knew it. So, I'm—"

"It was Chase," I cut her off. "He's taking Clint to court."

"Chase?" Her voice betrayed her shock. "Why would he do that?"

"It's a long story." I sighed and jumped to my feet. Cradling the cell phone between my ear and my shoulder, I headed for the closet as I considered my next words. Jude had grown silent. She knew better than to pester me for details in such matters.

I decided, even if I wanted to, there was no point in recapping yesterday's events. I had to talk with Chase first and ask him to redo his actions—and fast, before Clint made my life a living hell.

"Hold on a sec," I said to Jude and slipped into my jeans and shirt, regarding myself in the mirror.

In spite of the fact that I had never felt so tired, I looked radiant. Yeah, sex did that to you.

"So, you really met up with him?" Jude's question was fairly harmless, but the inquisitiveness in her voice was palpable.

I rolled my eyes, cursing the fact that I had loved every second with Chase—yet he had gone behind my back, as if the time we spent together meant nothing to him. "Yeah, I saw him all right."

"And?" Damn Jude and her curiosity.

"And we talked."

And I also slept with him.

Kissed him.

Begged him to lick me and take me while he pleasured me, and pleasure me again.

Relentlessly.

Oh, God.

The way he had fucked me slowly, hard, fast on the bed, in the shower, and on the floor, in that respective order, it had felt as though he couldn't get enough of me. But I couldn't admit that to Jude.

Not now.

Not ever.

Not when Chase spelled trouble with a six pack. Or was it an eight pack?

I couldn't tell her about the way he had pinned me underneath him, run his tongue along my neck, moved inside me so quickly I had let out a scream of delight. Nor could I tell her just how much I had enjoyed every minute of him inside me right before I fell asleep on top of him.

Why did I feel like a million bucks in spite of the fact that Chase might just be about to get me into real trouble with Clint? Obviously it couldn't be the sex. Or the fact that I was sore from the dozens of orgasms.

When I woke up at 2 a.m. to go to the bathroom, Chase was gone. The disappointment was brief, but compared to now it was nothing.

Glancing at my dishevelled bed, at the blankets and pillows that still smelled of him, I couldn't help but wonder if it had been a mistake to get involved with him.

What had I been thinking?

Obviously, if he looks like the devil, acts like the devil, it is the devil. Chase sure had the charm. His body was pure sin.

"Are you sure you're okay?" Jude asked cautiously. "You seem awfully still."

I laughed bitterly. "Would you sound okay if you harbored thoughts of killing your new husband?" I groaned again. "Jude, can we talk about this another time? I really have to see what Chase has to say on the matter."

"What about Clint?"

"Tell him I'll call him back."

"You better do that," she said. "He threatened you. I don't believe he was joking."

"Sounds exactly like Clint," I mumbled. "I've got to go. I'll call you as soon as I can."

"You promise?" Jude asked. "Because you already promised, and I waited all day and night for your call."

"I will. Bye." I ended the call and regarded myself in the mirror. My brown hair was a tangled mess, but my skin still carried the blush from last night, giving away just how much fun we had.

But the worst was my smile—my silly post-sex smile as pictures of my legs wrapped around Chase's naked body began to flash before my eyes.

"You crazy bastard," I whispered. "You really did it."

Clint had said there would be consequences. Knowing him, I wasn't stupid enough to believe otherwise. I had to take care of my interests first, if only to protect myself.

My phone beeped again. This time it was a text from Jude:

Forgot to ask. Do you want me to give you my attorney's contact details before you talk with Clint? I hired her last month to go over my work contract for my TV show. She's really good.

I shook my head. As if her employment contract lawyer could help me. What I needed now was someone to protect me mercilessly against Clint, someone who took no crap from anyone.

Knowing my stepfather and his lawyer, I needed a bulldog. A convincing, no bullshit, rabid bulldog.

Someone like…

I shook my head, then closed my eyes. I couldn't believe I had reached the point where I'd be saying what I was about to say. With a sigh, my hands flew over the touch screen as I typed the message to Jude.

No need. I already have a lawyer.

Chase would take care of the mess he had started. He had to.

***

My fist came hard against the wood as I rapped at the door. To a bystander, it probably looked like I was the raging wife about to confront her cheating husband and beat his mistress to a pulp. But the truth was I would have rather kicked Chase's ass for the mess he had caused me, and give the mistress a big fat kiss for stealing him from me.

Dressed in jeans and a white shirt, my hair still wet from the shower, and my lips painted in a demure shade of red, I hoped I looked civilized, but inside I was boiling. With every second that passed the anger inside me grew to immerse proportions, any feelings of euphoria from sex dissolving into thin air.

How dare he steal the contract and take Clint to court?

No surprise that Clint was angry. He had probably assumed I tricked him.

I knocked harder. "Open the fucking door, Chase," I shouted. "I know you're in there." It wasn't my imagination. The sound of the TV carried over from inside. At last, footsteps thudded.

The door opened slowly and a woman's pale face peered out.

My breath hitched and my heart stopped.

You know when I said I'd kiss the mistress?

Scratch that part.

She was beautiful. Like a real life doll, with flawless skin and big, blue eyes.

A towel was wrapped around her delicate body, and her long blond hair cascaded down her shoulders. "Yes?" Her accent was unmistakably foreign. Maybe Russian.

But her beauty wasn't what bothered me. She could have been butt ugly for all I cared.

What bothered me was the fact that she was in Chase's room, and judging from the dark smudges around her eyes—her only 'fault'—and the empty bottles of alcohol arranged on the bar, her night had been a fun one, too. The thought of her in Chase's bed, of him fucking her right after he had fucked me, made me fuming mad.

Had I not been enough for him?

How the fuck did he hook up with her so quickly after leaving my room, unless he had met her before and she had been waiting for him?

Something hard pierced my heart. Without thinking, I stormed past her into the room.

"Where is he?" I asked, taking notice of the unmade bed, the lacy underwear on the floor, and what looked like room service. In the background, I could hear the shower running.

Fucking hell.

First, he screwed me, then he went out to get dessert.

I should never have trusted him.

"Is he in there?" I asked.

She frowned, her eyes fixed on my lips as if she didn't quite understand me, her perfect plump lips pouting. "Who?"

"Chase."

"*Chase?*" she asked.

With my heart slamming against my chest, I headed for the door and grabbed the knob. As I was about to open it, a familiar voice echoed behind me.

"What are you doing?"

I stopped, my entire body going rigid, while I considered three scenarios that could play out:

a) Chase had a threesome and I was about to find out if the person in the shower was female or male.

I gulped down the horror stuck in my throat.

Oh, my god.

Please, don't let it be a threesome.

It was so far out of my sexual expertise that I couldn't even bare to think about it.

b) This was all in my head, and I was having a nervous breakdown. People were probably holding me down that instant while someone was calling for an ambulance.

c) I was in a dream from which I'd wake up any minute, which was very similar to b) and absolutely my ideal scenario.

I turned around to meet Chase's amused grin and the knowing glint in his eyes. He was standing in the doorway, holding two cups of coffee in his hands. The stunning woman eyed us both, confused.

"Chasse? Est-ce que tout va bien?" she asked again in her accent and he turned around to her.

"Tout va bien. I'm sorry. My wife confused the rooms," he explained to her. "She was actually looking for me."

My cheeks flamed.

"Oh." She let out a laugh, her finger going between her and him. "She thought you and I had une liaison passionnée."

As it happened, I knew that word.

She was French.

"Come on, Laurie." Chase winked. "I'll show you to my room."

My whole body burned with embarrassment as I

stormed past him and headed down the corridor with Chase chuckling behind me.

Chapter 19

AS SOON AS Chase closed the door behind us, I dropped onto his bed and covered my face with my hands, muttering, "Please kill me. This is so embarrassing."

"Quite the contrary, I think it's funny."

I dropped my hands onto the bed and stared up at the ceiling. "Easy for you to say. You're not the one who knocked on the wrong door."

He let out another sexy, roaring laugh and sat down next to me, the motion almost throwing me off the bed. My heart rejoiced, all too aware of the sudden closeness. As he leaned closer, far too close for comfort me, a whiff of his aftershave hit me, and I took a deep breath, eager to inhale his scent.

"You know," he whispered in my ear, "you were lucky I heard you down the hall and saved you a lot of trouble. God knows what might have happened if you opened the bathroom door and saw him naked. The poor guy would have been traumatized for life, thinking you were the wife and the divorce papers were basically lurking around the corner."

I had been yelling?

Earth, swallow me up whole!

"Just awesome." I groaned, which only had Chase laughing again. "What makes you think he was a cheater? Maybe that was his wife."

I turned to regard him. His fingers brushed my hair back out of my face gently and twisted a strand as his stunning eyes pierced mine. My body heated up under his touch.

"His wife's Indian. That was the paid help, if you get my drift."

I raised my eyebrows. "And your conclusion is based on what?"

"I'm psychic."

I rolled my eyes at his answer.

"Okay, I'll share my secrets," Chase said. "The picture frame on the nightstand was a dead giveaway. I don't know how you could miss it. It's like by bringing a family portrait with him, he felt less guilty fucking a stranger." He shook his head. "Anyway, you've got to admit, it makes a good story, though. As a lawyer, I've heard so many of those, it's ridiculous. I don't know why people get married, but don't keep it in their pants."

He sure knew what to say and when to say it.

It took all my willpower not to give in and kiss him—until he said the next stupid thing.

"That scene of yours—" He laughed. "And your face. Priceless."

"Oh, hilarious." I let out a sarcastic laugh as I rose on my elbows, facing him. "Enjoying yourself, aren't you? Why the fuck didn't you tell me where your room was?"

"You didn't ask." He kept grinning. "You just assumed. Out of interest, why didn't you knock on the door to your left rather than assume you got the door right? I mean, there was a fifty percent chance you got the door wrong. That's what usually crosses one's mind when a stranger opens."

"No idea." I began to chew my nail

Honestly, it was one of those brain dead, impulsive reactions, but I couldn't exactly tell him that when it came to him, any reasoning became non-existent. I decided to stick to parts of the truth. "Your brother headed in that direction, so I assumed..."

"Ah, my brother again." He shook his head, giving an exasperated sigh. "This is getting old, Laurie, you know? Let me guess, you still don't believe me that I had no idea he

227

was here?"

"Actually, I do now," I said.

His fingers twisted in my hair again, playing with a strand, pulling gently.

"What changed?" he asked absentmindedly, as though my hair was fascinating and he could barely focus on anything else. "Was it my excellent performance last night? Or this." He leaned forward and placed a kiss on my mouth, the unexpected motion both infuriating and intoxicating. For a moment, our tongues connected in that slow dance I loved. And then he pulled back again, leaving me breathless, wanting more.

Wanting him.

"No, it's the fact that I didn't find him in your room," I said, giving him a playful shove.

His heated gaze brushed my lips, then met my eyes, his glance going back and forth between the two, as if he considered whether to kiss me again.

"Je veux lècher chaque partie de ton corps," he said slowly, his tongue darting out to lick the corner of his mouth.

I stared at him, transfixed by his mouth, his tongue, the memory of the two so vivid I could almost feel his touch on my body, and a blush crept up my face.

I had no idea what he'd said, but it kind of sounded dirty.

And hot.

Hell, I loved it when he was dirty.

His eyes lingered on me for too long, reminding me of our sinfully sexy night and all the fun we had. His tongue brushed his lip skillfully, silently inviting me to play. There was no doubt he was focused on a lot of things—just not on a serious conversation.

I wanted a replay of last night so badly, I almost winced at the soft tug between my legs.

But there were more pressing issues to deal with, like Clint's phone call.

"What does this mean?" I asked, taking the bite, even though I should have known better.

"I could show you." He grinned, his eyes glinting with amusement, challenging me to take him up on his offer.

I shook my head. "There is no need to show off your linguistic skills."

"I could have sworn you were about to compliment them," he said smoothly.

"You already proved that last night."

And boy he did.

"That's right, baby." He grinned. "Je me suis beaucoup amuse."

"No idea what you said right now, so I'm going to pretend I didn't hear that one. We have far more important things to do than praise your tongue, and stroke your ego."

"Yeah? Like what?" His lips twitched. He ran a finger down my neck, and I shifted as another surge of wanting pulsed through me. "Like your jealousy issues? They were about to spiral out of control."

"I'm not jealous," I said, slightly defensive. I plucked a loose thread from the bedspread, unsure how to explain my motives. "I just thought you fucked someone hours after me."

My honesty surprised me. It also made me feel oddly self-conscious. After all, I knew how I sounded: insecure and yeah, jealous.

"Whoa. Let's stop there," Chase said. I raised my head and caught his hurt expression, my heart speeding up a little. "I'm offended that you think so lowly of me. Come on. What do you think I am? A sex addict? A cheater? We have a contract. I tend to respect those." He pressed a hand to his chest theatrically, which made me snort. "My reputation as your husband means a lot to me."

"Fine," I said, rolling my eyes. "I was ridiculous in my assumption."

He gestured with his hand, prompting for more. "And?"

"And what? Don't push it, Chase."

"You forget the most important fact: we're married," he said proudly, as if I was missing the most obvious thing. "That means in our relationship you won't ever have a reason to be jealous. I'm very committed to our cause."

What the hell was *our cause?*

"Being married has never stopped anyone from cheating," I mumbled.

"That might apply to a lot of people out there." He leaned closer. "But I only have eyes for you, baby."

"Says the guy who agreed to a pretend marriage and married me for my money without even knowing me."

"Which only shows my level of commitment." He brushed aside a strand of hair that clung to my cheek. "Have I ever disappointed you?"

I cocked my head. "Seriously? You're asking me that after I basically summed up our entire relationship?"

He waved his hand. "Yeah, let's leave aside the 'I married you for a reason' part. Other than that?"

His words had me silent.

I stared at him. A tenuous ball of fear formed in my belly as I remembered Jude's words. "Clint called today. How about that?"

"Good." He sighed and got up. "Let's grab some coffee."

"Good?" I frowned. "Is that all you have to say?"

He shrugged. "Well, what else do you want me to say? It was to be expected. That guy is about to lose all your inheritance and his business. Of course he's going to be mad. Next thing he'll appeal to your goodwill. Then he'll start threatening you. My advice?" He stared at me, his

231

playfulness gone, replaced with a thick layer of ice. "Tell him you're not interested in talking to him. That'll save us both time."

He stopped in the doorway, waiting for me to follow him. That's when I noticed the suitcases. I scanned his room. It was tidy—too tidy. It looked like he was about to move out.

"Are you leaving?" I asked. An unexpected pang of shock shot through me.

I met his gaze, and for the first time I noticed his face was cleanly shaven, his hair still wet.

"I'm going back to L.A.," he replied, his tone sober.

"When?"

"My plane leaves this afternoon."

"Because of Clint?"

Why did I feel faint? That he was leaving was the best thing that could have happened to me, and yet I wanted him to stay.

He nodded. "Yes. I need to get to work. It's going to be one of many trials."

"But I thought we couldn't leave for a week." My throat closed up. As he cocked his head, his lips drawn into a tight line, realization hit me.

He had lied to me.

The disappointment at having been lied to yet again hurt me, but not as much as the fact that he was about to leave

232

me. "I thought we were being honest with each other."

"I'm working on it," he said softly. "Would you have listened to my explanation if I told you I was only here to bail you out?"

He was right.

I wouldn't have.

"You ignored my wishes, Chase," I whispered. "I asked you not to go against him, but you went ahead with your plans. Why?"

He sighed and turned around. "I already told you that I don't have a choice. I owe this to my family." His footsteps thudded in the silence of the room. The bed moved under his weight as he sat next to me, only inches away.

"I owe it to my family, Laurie," he repeated. "Please, you have to understand. Don't you want your inheritance back?"

I fell silent. Did I want it back?

Waterfront Shore—the place had never been one of happiness. A place where I never had a father to grow up with, a place where my mom had killed herself.

Somehow, it didn't matter either way. It held no importance to me.

"What if I don't want it?" I asked, casting him a sideways glance. "Will that change anything?"

His lips tightened again. "I'm taking him to court. I'm going to fight for you, for us."

"My mom set up a Will, Chase. I'm not the heiress. You're going to lose."

"No, I won't," he said firmly. "Your grandparents were the sole owners at the time your mom died. Your mom would have been their heir, followed by you. If that won't win us the case, then her letters will."

"In her will, she wanted Clint to have all her money," I tried one more time. "There's no way her letters will say otherwise."

"How do know? Have you read them?" Chase asked, his tone challenging me.

His question rendered me silent for a moment. "No, but that's not the point. What matters is that I'm not interested in the money."

"This is crazy. You listen to your mom even though the law says you're entitled to a huge estate. The estate has been in your family for a long time. Why do you want to give it away to someone who ruins other people's lives?"

"Because my mom told me so." I almost choked on my breath. He was right, of course, but—

"You said she loved you," Chase continued. "Well, there's no love deeper than a mother's love for her child. I don't believe she was in the right frame of mind when she made that decision, which is why I've applied for an order to get access to her medical records."

I shook my head. "Stop talking as if you're doing it for

me," I whispered. "You're doing it for yourself. It's all about you and Kade."

He grew silent.

"I do care about you, Laurie." He intertwined his fingers with mine. "I'm not lying. I really like you. But the thing with Clint, it needs to be done. For my family's sake. I promised. I couldn't live with myself if I didn't do this. But I sure I cannot let you go."

I turned my head to him, marveling at the beautiful color of his eyes—the color of cloudy days and summer storms.

His words choked me up, brought tears to the back of my eyes.

"You're really serious about destroying Clint," I whispered, feeling weak as I took in his words. "Why didn't you warn me?"

"I told you yesterday."

"I thought I had time. Why didn't you tell me before, so I could prepare myself?"

"It wouldn't have served the purpose. Besides, I didn't know you well. I couldn't trust you." His gaze darkened. "Twelve months, Laurie. That's how long I need. After that, you can do what you want."

"Please," I whispered. "There's always a choice. You don't have to do it."

He sighed. "It's too late. I can't go back on my word."

In the silence of the room, I watched him stand and squeeze into his jacket. His broad shoulders looked amazing, just like every other inch of him.

"What do you mean?" I asked when his statement finally sank in. "We've been married for less than three days. How can it be too late?"

"Under the Inheritance Act, you're entitled to make an application to the court for an order," he said, pushing his hands into the pockets of his jeans. "As your husband, I have the same right as you, but as your lawyer I already applied for an order before we got married."

I felt faint. "How?"

"While you were busy with your wedding gown, I flew ahead and pulled a few strings to get things moving. You can't stop me, Laurie. I'm good at what I do, so don't even try."

I stared at him, stunned, my words failing me.

It made so much sense. Every single step had been a part of Chase's plan.

"You will understand," Chase said. "I don't expect you to forgive me, but I want you to know that I'm doing it for us. I'm doing it for your mom, too, because in all honesty, I believe she wanted you to be happy. She wanted you to have everything."

I kept staring at him. I couldn't wrap my head around Chase's words. My head was spinning. Everything was too much.

"What about us?" I asked weakly.

He took my hand in his. "We'll come out stronger."

I shook my head, both to deny his statement and to get rid of the tears stinging my eyes. "No." In spite of the earth-shattering sadness inside me, I smiled. It took all my willpower to do so. "Chase, I get what you have to do."

"I sense a but…"

I smiled again. "But I need to annul the marriage. There is no 'us.' There can't be. What you have to do…I understand, but I can't do it with you." I squeezed his hand. "Please let me go. There's no point in believing there could ever be more between us. My heart's not in it. It never will be. You're not the kind of person I'd ever want in my life."

Which was a lie. The pressure behind my eyes intensified. I had to finish this once and for all before I broke down and he saw through the mess inside me, right into my bleeding heart.

He stared at me for one hard moment.

"Laurie—"

"No, I'm serious. I want to annul it." I took a shaky breath and let it out. "You can have my inheritance. No hard feelings, but please, don't expect me to stay married to you. Please," I begged, closing my eyes. "Just sign the papers."

"You can't annul something you've consummated.

Besides, I can't," he whispered. "We have a contract."

My heart sank. "You can cancel it, Chase. No one forces you."

"I could but I don't want to," he said softly. "The risk is too great. In order to win, I need you to be my wife. I need the situation to be…"

"Convincing." I nodded. "I understand, but I don't want to live with you."

"Why are you doing this?" he asked.

I closed my eyes, feeling despair, hopelessness, and sadness washing over me. "I can't live with you. I can't see you every day." I opened my eyes again.

"Why?" Chase asked. "There are so many things I want for us. I want to wake up next to you. I want to see you every day. I won't let the past break us apart."

I shook my head again. "I cannot deal with the pressure, nor a trial. I cannot face it. You'll never be the person I—"

I fell in love with.

I broke off, keeping that part to myself.

"No," he said forcefully. "I want to know why you want to stay away from me."

"Because…" I struggled choosing my words. "I can't get involved with you again."

"Why?"

"Because I don't want to get more emotionally attached than I already am. Okay? Stop asking me such questions, I can't answer them," I said angrily. "Just accept that I wouldn't be proud of myself."

"Laurie." He sounded genuinely shocked. "I won't give you a divorce."

"Yet," I added.

"No." He shook his head. "I won't agree to a divorce at all. Not now, not tomorrow, nor when the trial's over."

I stared at him. "Why?"

"I don't want to lose you." His words came out low, and for a moment I wasn't sure I had heard him right.

I frowned. "Look, you don't have to lie, Chase. It was a business proposition. Nothing more. You wanted revenge, I wanted the letters. There is no need for you to pretend that there was more between us."

"I don't think you understand what I'm saying." His lips swept over my cheek, his nose brushing mine, as he whispered in my ear, "When I said I like you, what I really meant isn't that I want to fuck you, or that we're great friends. I'm saying that I really want to be with you. Every minute I see you, I fall in love with you even more, and I know you can feel it, too. Don't pretend there's nothing between us because you're lying to yourself."

I shook my head. A tear trickled down my cheek. "What we had was nice, but it wasn't real. None of this is."

"What about our feelings?" he asked, moving back.

Our feelings.

I smiled bitterly.

Not real.

Not his feelings, nor mine.

"I don't know about you, but I don't want to love." I looked up at him. "As for you, if you really love me, if only a little bit, you'll let me go. You'll stop asking to see me. You'll stop contacting me."

"You're only saying that because you're not ready," he said.

I shook my head. "No, Chase. Please listen to what I'm telling you. I don't want to love you. What we have—had—will pass. There's no point in believing there could ever be more. That…" I broke off, the pain too heavy.

For a long moment, there was silence.

"Okay," he said. His expression was pained, but it was nothing compared to what I was feeling inside. "Okay." His fingers settled beneath my chin, forcing me to meet his gaze. "I'm going to let you go, Laurie, but I want you to know that I'll be waiting for you. I'll wait until you're ready for my love." I pulled away but he didn't let go. "Twelve months. That's how long it'll take me to get your inheritance back."

"Twelve months," I repeated. "In twelve months I want my divorce. Until then…"

"I'll stay away if that's what you want."

"That's what I want, Chase. No contact. I don't want to

hear from you again."

His jaw set, but he said no more. He let go of me. I used the opportunity to get up and walk past him, closing the door behind me.

Chapter 20

THE MOMENT I slammed the door behind me, a first ripple escaped my throat. Pressing a hand against my mouth to stifle the sound, I headed for the bathroom and locked up behind me.

It was the only place where I knew Chase wouldn't hear the silent cries.

It was the only place where I felt it was safe to let out my emotions.

To escape the pain I was feeling. When I had asked for a divorce, every part of me broke. It broke in the knowledge that I had fallen in love with him, and that no matter what I said or did, I wasn't important to him. He wanted his revenge, and once he got it, I'd be a part of his past.

In spite of his claims, I was a tool he'd discard of once he didn't need it any more.

Stripping off my clothes, I stepped inside the small cubicle and turned on the water, the coldness seeping into my skin.

It was going to be hard, but between the choice of seeing Chase every day, feeling the pain of knowing he'd never love me the way I loved him, and the choice of staying away, feeling the pain of his absence, I knew I'd rather go for the latter.

I sunk to my knees, burying my face in my hands, and let the water pound against my naked body in the hope it could wash away the pain, the love, my soul.

I didn't know how long I just sat there, stuck in that one place where my dreams had been crushed, and I was forced to face the harsh reality that I had been a pawn in Chase's game.

Eventually, the crying ebbed, and I forced my shivering body into an upright position.

I forced myself to take slow steps toward the mirror and face the woman I had become.

Her reflection stared at me, her eyes hard, unforgiving, as if she was questioning my decision.

"Shut up," I whispered to her and wrapped a towel around my shivering body, then returned to my room to change.

243

Everything felt empty now that I knew Chase would be gone. He didn't say when he'd be leaving, but my heart was already missing him like crazy. A few times, I caught myself glancing toward the door in the hope he'd magically appear and tell me his plans had changed.

That's when I noticed the piece of paper on the floor.

Chase. I knew it was from him.

I dashed for it, my breathing trapped in my chest, as I lifted the paper to read the beautiful cursive.

Laurie,

I don't want to part like this. Please meet me at the beach.

The driver's waiting for you downstairs. If you don't want to come, I'll respect your wishes. You'll get your divorce papers nonetheless.

I promise.

-C

No xox. No love. Nothing. Only a simple word: promise.

Promise could mean a lot of things in Chase's world. It could also mean nothing.

I couldn't go. Of course, I couldn't.

It was out of the question. And yet my heart longed to see him one more time. After all the crying, I felt as if the worst was over. I had accepted that things were over, that nothing would change his mind, that he'd sign the divorce papers after the twelve months were over, that things between Clint and I would never be the same again after what Chase was about to do—not that they were great to begin with.

I retrieved my phone from where I had left it on the bed and scrolled through my missed calls. Clint's number showed up a few times. Sitting down, I speed-dialed his number, my pulse spiking.

"Hi, Clint." My voice sounded different. Strangled. Defeated. As if a part of me had died.

"Lauren." His fake voice echoed down the line. "How's my favorite girl doing?"

I cringed at his choice of words. It wasn't like he had a few daughters.

"I'm good."

A pause, then, "Where are you? I'd like to talk to you."

"I'd rather do this over the phone."

Another heavy pause.

"Why are you making things difficult for me?" His tone was still friendly, but underneath I could hear the anger, the accusation. "I raised you as the good daughter you are and how are you repaying me? You steal the contract we had and go behind my back to file a court order. Now, don't deny it. I know you're behind it. It's okay. You can admit it,

245

and I promise I'll forgive you. But right now, I need you to stop those childish antics and withdraw—"

"It wasn't me," I cut him off.

"What?"

"I didn't steal the contract."

"But you know what's going on," he said matter-of-factly. "You're a clever girl. I don't have to tell you that going against me won't bring your mother back."

My grip on my phone tightened. "How come you never say her name? In all the years since she's been dead, you never once said her name."

I let out a wry laugh as the realization dawned on me.

"Of course I know Eleanor's name. You know how much I loved her. I think of her every day."

"You're lying," I said. "You never told me what happened the day she died. You never told me what happened to her. It's like she never existed. All the years, I spent at Waterfront Shore, it was like I never had a mother."

"It's because her memory's too painful."

"You knew her for only two years, Clint," I said dryly.

"In spite of her mental illness, she was still the most beautiful woman I've ever met."

His words touched me. They made me incredibly sad. But there was something calculating about the way he said them. Like he had practiced them.

"Is it true, did you destroy other people's lives?" I asked. "Did you convince people to invest their money in their business before you took everything away from them?"

The silence lasted for a second. "What does that have to do with my estate?"

Not *your* estate or *the* estate.

My estate.

"You mean my mother's estate?" I asked. "The estate that had been in my family for generations before you came along?"

"You know it's mine. It's what your mother wanted."

"Did she?" I asked.

The silence was short, the reply hateful. "What are you talking about? Your mother was mentally ill, but she wanted me to have the estate."

"Exactly." I nodded, for the first time really seeing Chase's point. "Was she even able to make a rational decision?"

"I don't know what you're getting at, but I swear, I'll crush you."

The threat was there, not veiled. Plain and simple.

"We'll see," I said.

"You greedy bitch," Clint said. "I agreed to give you one quarter of the inheritance, and that's how you repay me? You don't deserve it. You hear me? If you don't drop the case, I'm going to make you pay."

I hung up, my fingers trembling at his harsh words.

It didn't take long before the phone began to ring.

I counted the calls as I put on clean clothes. By the third time Clint called, I was long gone.

Chapter 21

I FOUND HIM on the beach. It was a beautiful place, I had to give him that. Much less crowded than I had expected, and so close to the hotel. He was sitting on the white sand, his eyes fixed on the horizon. He didn't turn his face to me as I dropped down next to him, stretching out my legs as far as I could. The water was sparkling blue, beckoning to me to take a swim, if only this vacation hadn't turned out quite so unexpected. If only I didn't know Chase was about to leave.

For a while, we sat there, the hot Mexican sun warming my skin, but not quite reaching my heart.

Chase spoke first. "I didn't think you'd come."

"Surprised me, too."

He nodded, his eyes absent. "You haven't changed your

mind, have you?"

My eyebrows rose. "About what?"

"About us living together. You know, going back to NY together."

I shook my head, then sighed. "No, Chase."

"Laurie," he whispered. "I don't want to lie—"

"Then don't." I looked away because his eyes were too beautiful. Too damn convincing.

"You'd never understand."

I smiled bitterly. "Trust me, I do. You and Kade need revenge, and I so happen to be the collateral damage. But here's what I don't get. What's in it for you when all is said and done? I really hope it'll be worth it."

"It's not just revenge, Laurie," Chase said. "Clint destroys people. He needs to be stopped. I think I've made myself clear on that part."

I sighed again and watched the waves roll in, but the serenity of the setting didn't quite manage to calm the raging storm inside me. "I know. I talked with him earlier."

"And?"

"I told him it's on. That's why I'm here." He looked at me surprised, and I felt the need to clarify. "I want you to go ahead and do what needs to be done."

"That means a lot to me." He grabbed my hand, his eyes meeting mine. "I promise you as soon as Clint loses his money, it'll all be transferred to you. No harm done."

I chuckled darkly. "No harm done, huh? What about my feelings, Chase? I thought we had a real thing going on." I turned to him and caught the imploring glint in his eyes. "You really think I came here because I might be afraid of losing money? Honestly, I don't care about that at all. It's the other matter that bothers me."

His expression changed from surprise to disbelief.

"Are you saying you feel more?" he asked quietly.

"More?" I laughed through the curtain of tears clouding my vision. "I feel everything. I feel the sun in my eyes when I look at you. I smell the sky when you breathe. I don't call this nothing. I call it everything."

"Then leave with me." His plea surprised me, his intensity made me want to pack my bags and follow him to the end of the world and back. "I can arrange a seat for you."

"I can't," I whispered. "Even if I wanted to, I can't. What I said earlier, I meant it."

His eyes widened. "You want—"

I nodded. "I still want a divorce."

"Why?" There was so much sadness in his eyes, my heart felt like it was going to burst from the weight of my pain. "Why would you give us up? You know that I want to give us a try."

"Because I can't deal with it." I looked at him. "You got what you wanted. Me. And your revenge. But now I need to move on. For my sake, for our sake. Because what we have is not real. It's—"

His hand touched my face. I didn't even have time to take a breath before his lips came crashing down. They ripped open a hole in my heart, filling it with the sweet promise of something I knew would be gone in the blink of an eye.

Not with desire, not with anger, not with hope, but love.

Love for this man I barely knew.

Love for someone who couldn't love me as much as I did him.

Or at least that was what I thought.

"It feels pretty real to me," Chase whispered against my lips.

"It's unrealistic," I whispered. "You fell in love with your target. You honestly believe it'd ever work out?" I inched closer, barely able to stifle the need to throw myself into his arms and trust him with my heart I knew I could never give him. "I want things to be different. I want there to be an *us*, but life doesn't work that way. I hate to say it, but your brother's right."

His mouth tightened. My answer didn't please him.

"I care about you, Laurie," he whispered. "I really do. But—"

"But what?"

"I've never let anybody be this close to me. My brother

says I'm incapable of love. That's what everyone told me, and I believed them. That's why it was easy to go on with my plans, and why I suggested that I do it rather than Kade. But after meeting you, something inside me changed." My breath hitched at his words. "It was easy to make myself believe that it was only a job, that I could move on after the deed was done, but now—" His glance searched mine in a long, tender moment. "—now I'm not sure that I'll ever be able to stay away from you. I don't think I want to. You have come to mean so much to me."

I let out a breath I didn't know I was holding. "What are you saying, Chase?"

"I'm a lawyer. I've been taught not to let my feelings interfere and all that bullshit. But with you I feel that I can be myself. I feel that something is happening between us. I think that's why I can't stay away from you."

"Why?"

His hands cupped my face and his thumbs brushed my cheeks. "You know the answer."

"I want to hear it."

He sighed. "I'm falling in love with you, and there's nothing I can do to stop it."

The falling in love part again. The first time he had said it I made myself believe it was just a lie. Now I wasn't so sure about it.

"You make it sound like it's a bad thing," I whispered.

He remained silent as he turned his attention to the ocean. "It is if you keep insisting that you want a divorce. How are we supposed to grow as a couple when you want me to stay away from you."

"We can't ever be a couple, Chase," I said with more fervor than I felt.

He shook his head, suddenly angry. "I can. It's you who can't so please speak for yourself. If things were different, if I didn't have to do what I have to do about Clint—"

"Then I'd date you for real," I whispered. "I'd want to be with you, but this…what we have now…what you have to do for yourself….it can't work. You know it. It's just not possible. I can't forgive you."

My eyes filled with tears, but they didn't flow.

He frowned. "Are you implying that you're ready to date others?"

"It means you're free to do what you want to do. If you fuck others, you're free to do so." I threw him a sideways glance, my heart both burning and bleeding at the thought.

"I can't do that."

I smiled. "You can. You will."

"The feelings I have for you won't let me."

"Give it a few months and you'll change your mind," I said bitterly.

"Can we stay in touch during the trial?" Chase asked. The change in topic didn't escape my attention, but I let it pass. "It doesn't even have to be face to face."

"No."

"Laurie," he whispered. "Just because I'm helping my brother and just because I don't want to be in love with you doesn't mean we shouldn't see each other."

"I can't do it." I shook my head more firmly than I wanted. "It's not healthy for us." I met his fiery glance as I continued, "Work out what you have to do. If by the end of it you still feel strongly for me, let me know. But until then, there's not a chance in hell for us. Trust me, it's better this way. It's better for us. I need the distance, and you need it, too." I forced a weak smile to my lips. "If you love me like I love you, please let me go, but not before—" My words died on my lips, my voice quivering.

"What can I do?"

I smiled again. "Make love to me. Give me something before you go."

"Fine." His fingers curled around mine and he helped me up. "Let's be clear. I won't give up on you. Irrespective of what you think, my feelings for you are real. The sooner you accept it, the better."

"Don't make promises." I lifted on my toes to place a kiss on his lips. "Make sure to remember me."

He tasted of summer and wind, of the kind of sweet happiness I could never have.

I smiled even though inside I was breaking.

Whatever we had, it was about to come to an end.

Today would be the last time I'd see him. I'd kiss him one last time before he'd move on. Find someone else. Someone more beautiful. More like him. Someone who'd help him forget me.

"I will, Laurie," he whispered. "I'll always remember you."

Chapter 22

I HAD ALWAYS believed in first love. Chase had been my first love. What I didn't believe was that first love ever lasted. Chase would move on, I was sure of that. I was also sure that fairy tales only existed in movies and books. That it was all in my mind—the emotions, albeit contradictory ones, the wavering decision not to go after him while forcing myself to stay.

When I had told Chase I wanted a divorce, I had been sure I was doing the right thing for us. That I'd be avoiding the awkward breakup that always comes no matter how great a relationship is at the beginning.

Had I made the wrong decision?

It was early afternoon when Chase left. I could still feel his kiss on my forehead; I could still hear the steps when he departed, and the sound of the door when it closed after him.

Pretending to be asleep was much easier than I anticipated. I wanted to avoid the awkward goodbye, the awful silence, and the embarrassing moment of having to stop my tears from falling, but not quite being able to. I thought saying goodbye before his actual departure and then seeing him leave would be easy, and yet I realized nothing about Chase was ever easy.

I had wanted to remember him the way I had come to know him: as Mystery Guy.

A guy with so many secrets he deserved his own mystery novel.

A man who had made me laugh, who had given me a special time to remember him by, who had made me trust him, open up to him. In spite of the lies he had told me, he'd always be in my heart.

As soon as the door closed, I willed myself to sleep, if only to stop the tears and the pain.

When I woke up again, evening was falling and the sun was setting on the horizon. Ignoring the pain in my skull, I forced myself to my feet when my gaze fell on the tiny note on Chase's side of the bed.

It read:

I've left something for you at reception.

Consider it my parting gift.
Your husband

I pressed the note to my chest. Whatever Chase wanted me to have, it could wait. I wasn't yet ready for more tears. It was hard enough that my room, the pillows, even my shirt, smelled of him. It was bad enough to know that the bed I was lying on was the one where we had made love. And it wasn't just the room—it was everything about me, as if a part of him had remained behind, attaching itself to me in the form of memories, thoughts, feelings. I could almost see him standing to my left, sporting the most beautiful smile on his face while telling me what to wear. Peering to my right, I remembered the way he had kissed me on that spot before he pulled me into his arms with a fervor that had left me breathless.

It felt as though an entire week had passed, instead of hours. Already I missed our banter, his smile, everything about him. I peered at the time on my cell phone. By now his plane had taken off, returning him to a life that didn't involve me.

Calling Jude was the right thing to do. Luckily, she sensed my inner turmoil instantly and stopped asking questions.

"When are you coming home?" she asked.

"Probably tomorrow."

"And Chase?" She hesitated, as though she didn't know whether he was a subject she could bring up. I could sense her discomfort in her delayed question.

"Don't worry about him." For the first time in my life, I didn't try to hide the sadness in my voice. "He left. It's better this way."

The toxic tears from before began to build up in my eyes. It took all my willpower not to give in and break down. As if sensing it, Jude changed the subject, fake cheerfulness infused into her tone.

"Hey, I can't wait to see you again," she said. "I've heard of this yoga center that we need to check out. It's supposed to be super cheap and great for you. I also bought the new Walking Dead season on DVD."

"Great." I smiled, missing her so much. "Did you have a sneak peek?"

"What kind of friend do you take me for?" she asked. "You know I'd never do something like that without you."

I smiled, feeling grateful for the fact that when I returned to L.A. someone would be there for me.

Jude was right. She was my family. The only family I ever had. There was nothing I wouldn't have given up for her.

"My flight's tomorrow," I said.

"You promise?"

I laughed through the curtain of tears blurring my

vision. "You can bet on it."

I ended the call quickly and began to plan the last day of my short vacation. The return flight ticket had to be booked so I called the reception area to inquire about available tickets.

Packing my things kept me busy for an hour or two. It had been a short vacation, but I felt different. Wiser. I had grown as a person. I finished up, leaving my bikini on the bed, deciding to visit the beach one last time, even though without Chase it wasn't going to feel the same.

Once everything was packed, I headed downstairs.

"I hope you had a pleasant stay at Casa Estevan," the receptionist said. It was the same one who had greeted me upon my arrival. Her hair was still bleached, and her eyebrows looked still horrible, but her smile—it looked genuine and caring.

"Thank you. It was the best."

"I'm so glad to hear." She handed me the info leaflet. "Here's your flight information. I made sure to print everything out."

"Thank you. I'll be checking out tomorrow morning." I flicked through the leaflet, and then pulled out my credit card. "How much is this going to be?"

"Your husband settled the bill this morning." She smiled. "He also said to charge his card with your return flight and pay for the driver as long as you need him. And he left you this." She kept her back turned on me as she retrieved a small box from a drawer, and then pushed it toward me. "He says it's your birthday gift."

My heart plunged. "Thank you."

Once inside the safety of my hotel room, the heavy sadness inside me became unbearable. I suppressed the urge to run my hands over the pillow he had slept on, but I couldn't quite fight the urge to hold on to that tiny memory of him.

Slowly, I leaned over the pillow and inhaled his scent. I knew I didn't have to. The whole room still smelled of him. He seemed to be everywhere. Inside my heart. On my skin. In my thoughts.

And yet it wasn't enough.

I leaned back on the bed.

My throat made a choked sound as another wave of pain rippled through me.

His parting gift—a white box with a turquoise ribbon—lay in my lap. No note was attached to it.

I opened it.

As soon as I lifted the lid, a shaky breath escaped my lips.

The first thing that caught my attention was the necklace—my mom's necklace arranged on a black velvet pillow. My fingers shook as I lifted it up in the air. The amethyst, crowned by a Sterling silver Celtic design, sparkled in the sun. I realized Chase had kept true to his word. The loose stone had been fixed.

"Thank you," I whispered, even though he was miles away and couldn't hear me.

I had almost stashed away the box when I realized it was far too big and heavy. With a frown, I removed the lid and let out another shaky breath as my eyes fell on the letters and the familiar handwriting.

For Laurie.

It was my mother's handwriting, without a doubt.

My breath made a whizzing sound as tears started flowing down my cheeks.

Oh, my God.

Chase got the letters. I had no idea how he did it, but it was amazing. When Clint called, I had been afraid he'd never give them to me. That he'd break his promise. I smiled as I realized all my fears had been unwarranted. Chase had picked them up for me. Gratitude and happiness settled within my heart, and for a moment I considered calling him to tell him just how grateful I was.

But that thought was quickly lost when I realized the magnitude of the situation.

My mom's letters were mine. Finally.

A shaky breath escaped my lips as I stacked them together and lifted them to my face, inhaling their scent. They felt so old, fragile, but I could smell the lavender and *her*. A tear rolled down my cheek as my feelings erupted, leaving me a sobbing mess of joy and sadness.

At last, I scanned through them. There were only four of them—each of them had a few inscribed words at the back.

They said:

For Laurie when she has her first child.
For Laurie when she feels sad.
For him.

I frowned at the third letter, surprised that my mother had left a letter for Clint, but then of course she would. She had married him. There had to be a lot she never got to say.

My eyes fell on the last letter. The fourth one was much thicker than the other letters. It said:

Laurie, open me first after your twenty-third birthday.

It was directed at me, and so much thicker and larger than any other letter. A short shake, and I knew there was something inside. Pictures? A postcard?

My heart sped up as I let my finger trail over the familiar handwriting. I took my time opening it. When I finally did,

I reread it a few times, and then I cried myself to sleep, feeling that my world had gone the darkest shade of black.

"Oh, my God," I whispered, my voice choked, ready to die in my chest.

It made so much sense.

Everything I thought I knew had been crushed by her words.

Chapter 23

Eleanor's Letter

This is for you, my daughter—the only thing I've really truly loved, like every mother should her child.

The day I'm writing this letter, you're nine years old. In a few weeks, you'll turn ten. I want you to get this letter when you're twenty-three, maybe even older. By that time, at least thirteen years will have passed, and you'll be a beautiful, intelligent woman.

You most certainly have many questions. There's a great deal of information in this letter. Do not feel you have to understand everything at once. Some of what I will reveal will be hard to believe. Maybe you'll be angry. Please ignore everything that you're not ready to accept until you feel the right time has come. Understand, too, that I'm a human being. I made mistakes. I didn't always know what's right and what's wrong.

My biggest fear is that, some of the things in this letter will make you judge me. Again, please know that I only want you to understand who I am, what happened to me, what I had to do. The truth is, much of what I've done was a mistake. I had no friends to help me see the truth. I had no one I could confide in. There was no one to teach me faith. I didn't know better.

One of the reasons I sent you to boarding school was that I hoped you'd never be alone. I wanted you to discover the blessing of friendship. I wanted you to learn the earthy, practical things in life rather than be homeschooled, and at the constant mercy of others. I couldn't let you make the same mistakes I made, and most of all, I couldn't let you witness my gradual mental decline.

Clint has without a doubt told you that I was insane. It's a lie we concocted together...a means to hide the fact that my illness takes away my memories and makes everyday tasks impossible. My illness has started to transform me into someone I'm not. I've become someone I no longer recognize. Sometimes I think of the loss of my memory as a blessing, but then I remember that I'm also losing myself, that I forget how to be a mother to you, that all the good things will be erased, too, and I realize just how much of a loss I'm about to suffer.

In the beginning, we were hopeful, thinking the medication I was

267

prescribed would take care of my little problem, but now we know my illness cannot be cured. The doctors have told me that it's only a matter of time until I lose my memory, the ability to breathe, eat, and I'll die. They tell me I have months left, but I don't feel like I have months. I feel like it can happen any time now, which is why I've been up for thirty-six hours to draw up my Last Will and the letters.

So, please forgive me if the words seem jumbled or hard to understand. It's not my intention. I'm just trying not to sleep and forget. If I fall asleep, I've no idea in what state I'll be when I wake up, and days, even weeks could pass before I remember what I was about to do before my memory failed me.

I want to start from the beginning, what I deem the most important events first.

My name is Eleanor Hanson and I'm your mother. I was born Eleanor Stonefield to John Stonefield and Annette Fiddling. Your father is Richard Walker. Moving on from him was hard. Indeed, it took me a few years, but you were the one thing that kept me sane. You were a gorgeous baby, my love, my joy. Everything was easier with you. But living so close to your grandparents wasn't. I'm not proud of who my parents are. I'm not proud of what they've done to me.

My father was a hard and strict man. My mother was very religious. You will know very little about them. That's because I made sure you wouldn't get to know them.

I wouldn't say that my parents were evil, but they were cruel people. Every parent who harms a child should not be called a parent but a monster.

I cannot explain the pain I went through whenever they punished me as a child, each in their own way. Though I'm sure my parents loved me, they both turned a blind eye, abandoned me when I needed them the most. My mother knew what was happening to me. I confided in her early on. Yet, she proclaimed that it was all in my head. My father had this tendency to sweep everything under the rug to keep the family name untarnished.

The truth is, I didn't know that being sexually abused by your uncle is wrong, until I got much older and had you. As a child, I assumed I had no choice and that I had to accept my family for who they were. As I grew older, I knew I needed to escape. Marriage was my only way to get away from them all.

That my uncle raped me throughout my childhood and adolescence is not something I'm proud of. In fact, I wished I didn't have to tell you, but if it opens your eyes to the world I lived in, then so be it. I hope it'll help you understand some of the choices I made in my life.

There's something else I need to tell you. Something that's even harder to put on paper. Something I still cannot live with, even after all those years.

My tears are falling as I write this, and I have to be very careful not to stain the paper.

You have a half brother. That's when my parents could no longer deny the obvious. I was fifteen years old when they sent me to a monastery to bear my uncle's child. I was left afraid and alone among strangers, so my parents' rich friends wouldn't find out. Among strangers I learned to feel safe until the day I was forced to give up my child.

I prayed. I pleaded with them to allow me to keep my son, but nothing I said could make them see my pain. Even to this moment, I still think of him. I miss him every day. The three days I had him might not seem like a lot, but they were the best of my life, until I had you.

In that short time I dared not sleep out of fear that I would miss a single moment with him.

Giving him away was the hardest thing I've ever done, much harder than the sexual abuse I had endured. After nine months of carrying him, I loved him more than I loved myself. I loved him and his innocence in spite of my hatred for the despiteful man who was his father. You don't know how hard it is to give away a part of your heart until you experience it.

I cannot state how many tears I have shed about my broken family, or how many times I thought of killing myself.

As I'm writing this, my boy should be sixteen. He's seven years older than you. By the time you get the letters, he'll be almost thirty. The name I chose for him is Kaiden—Kaiden Stonefield—though his new parents might have changed his name.

I don't know where he's living, but I can feel him in my heart. Like I can feel you in my heart. Two children, both linked by my blood and womb.

I pray he's with a good family. If I could tell him that I would never have given him away out of free will, I would. I would hate him to think his mother didn't want him because she didn't love him when the opposite is the truth.

Having a real family has always been my dream. Ever since I was a child, I wanted to be a mother. When you were born, I was older, wiser. I knew you couldn't replace Kaiden, but you filled a big hole in my heart that your brother had left behind.

My God, Laurie. I was so happy when I held you in my arms the

271

first time. You had the tiniest hands and feet. Born with the cord around your neck, the doctors were sure you would never breathe. But as I was holding you in my arms, my tears staining your little face, my fear that I would lose my next child paralyzing me, I whispered, "Breathe, Laurie, breathe for me."

And you did. You did it for me. And when you opened your eyes and looked at me, I knew I would love you forever. I knew I would never give you up, no matter what happened. That I would protect you with my life because you were my little girl.

I was so afraid that the same history would repeat itself and what happened to me would happen to you. I could trust no one. It's one of the reasons I married Clint. You needed a father figure. And I needed to get away from my family.

Only a few people know what happened to me: my parents, Clint, your father. The truth was, my life was a complete lie to everyone else. I met your father when I was seventeen. He was my first friend. He was also my first love. He was also the first lie I told you. I hope you'll find it in your heart to forgive me that I claimed we were married before he died. None of that is true.

He isn't who you think he is. He's not an honorable man nor is he someone with a good heart. They were lies I told you to protect you from the truth. Lies I told myself to help me move on. When he got me pregnant, our parents insisted that we marry. When the day came, he ran off and left me behind. As a child, you wouldn't have understood, but now that you're older, I hope you can feel the heartbreak he caused me. Lies are not honorable, but sometimes when the truth is too painful and we have no choice, we have to lie. I think I mostly lied to myself and I got to a point where I began to believe my own lies.

As far as I know, your father is still alive. I wish I could tell you that he loved you and wanted to see you, but the truth is he's always been a coward who feared my father.

I tried to contact him on many occasions. I told him about you. I sent him photos. But he never replied. In my heart, I wanted to believe he loved me for a long time, that something or someone held him back, but the truth is, he wasn't in love with me. I wouldn't be surprised if he thought I was a rich, spoiled, and strange young woman. At some point, I even believed that my father paid him off to be my friend. That's the downside of being rich—you never know if anyone ever likes you for who you are.

Choose your friends carefully. Most of them will run when the going gets rough. Most of them would rather take the money than stick around. I can't blame your father, though. He was younger than I was when I found out that I was pregnant with you. He wasn't ready to be a father. He wanted to be a physician, study, travel the world, and that's exactly what he achieved.

If you decide to contact him, I have included everything about him below, though you should know that he is now married with children.

I married Clint because I wanted to be loved rather than hurt. Even though I've never been in love with him, I've always respected him for who he is. Before we married, he chased me for years and taught me that I could rely on him.

Now that you know my story, you will see that my life's been a lie for a long time. I've been carrying too many secrets. The burden has become too heavy to bear.

If you're angry with me, please know, I still love you.

I've decided that money should not define you. I don't want you to be used. I don't want people to hurt you or rob you blind just because you were born who you are. Your wealth won't help you make many real friends and so I've decided to keep your rightful money away from you until you become the open-minded, independent individual with a fixed set of opinions I know you will be. Once that is achieved, my duty as your mother has been accomplished.

My twenty-third birthday was an important year for me. It was the year I conceived you. It was the year I grew. It was the year I met Clint and we became friends. It was the year I realized that I'm responsible for my own life, that no one can hold me down. It's also the year my parents asked me for forgiveness after my uncle died.

While Clint is not the man I love, he is my safety net. He offered me a chance to get away from my family. He treated me well. He wanted to be your father. I don't know many men who would have jumped in wholeheartedly at the idea of raising someone else's child. Because my mind is deteriorating I have asked him to take over my business. I have asked him to take good care of you. And when I told him that I'd mention him in my Will, I made him promise that he would give you the estate once you were old enough.

Whether he will keep his promise is a different matter. I would like to believe it, but honestly, my life has taught me that I cannot trust anyone.

So I did something to protect you. I made a Last Will to overrule the previous one. You will find it in this letter.

I feel bad for Clint. I feel bad for not trusting him, but it's the only way to ensure I'll be able to take care of you after my death. Until the day you inherit everything, Clint will be your legal guardian. If not him, then who else? I have no sisters or brothers. My father is still alive, but I would rather give you to Clint than to him. At least I know Clint will take good care of you.

In my first will I'll ask you to give up your inheritance, and for a very good reason. I want you to go to college and experience life like any other young woman out there. I want you to learn the value of friendship and happiness without the heavy burden that wealth brings with it. You shall receive everything when you're old enough to make your own, wise decisions. While I know Clint loves me, I'm not naïve enough to trust that he'll hold on to me forever. Someday he will move on, like your father did.

I cannot take the risk that he will become greedy.

My last Will and Testament that will be read upon my death will state that Clint gets everything, even though he and I have a verbal agreement that you're to receive everything when you turn twenty-three regardless of who you've become. To make sure you find out about the existence of these letters, I've included a clause that requires you to be attached by the time you turn twenty-three years old. The reason is that I want you to be with someone who loves you for who you are rather than the money you'll inherit.

Should Clint break his promise to me, my last Will is inside this letter. It's co-signed by Nurse Marla and our gardener. It's the only copy I have and they are the only witnesses, so make sure you don't lose it. I also have included their contact details below.

Marla has always been good to me. She is also the closest I've ever come to having a real friend who hasn't betrayed me. I've asked her to keep some things from me for you. Make sure to contact her. While she does not know about my past, she knows about my heartbreak that I've experienced at the hands of your father, and she understands what I have to do.

No one is perfect, Laurie. No one can be completely faultless. Not I, not my parents, not my uncle, nor Clint. It's part of being human. Important is what you do with your faults, and what you can live with. In the end, it's your life and your decision what you make of it. My decision was to make sure that I did the opposite of what I experienced in life. I don't know why I'm writing this. Maybe because the hardest thing is yet to come.

I know you will hate me for this. I would, too, but I have to do it, Laurie. It's not your fault, nor Clint's. It's also not my father's fault. Nor my mother's. It's my own. I've considered this for a long time now. Today, my thoughts are lucid. Today that I can speak clearly, I know I have to do it. I don't want to die at the clinic, labeled a mentally ill person. I want to do it on my own terms, as someone who's aware of what she does.

Please forgive me.

I cannot stand to see myself slipping away. My mind...it's not what it used to be. On some days, I don't recognize myself. Those days become more and more frequent. I wander off with absolutely no idea of who I am, where I lived, what I do. On those days, I forget to eat, I forget that I exist. On some days, I wake up with wounds I inflict upon myself. This is not a way to live. I do not want to forget. I want to live, and be in control of myself, and if I cannot be that way, I would rather die as long as I know you exist.

Memory can be a precious thing, my daughter. I took it for granted, until I started to forget a little each day. The good memories were the first ones to go. I can feel it.

The medication I take isn't helping. It makes my nightmares worse. It keeps me stuck in the past. I'm telling Clint that I'm taking it, but the truth is, I haven't for weeks. I do not want to burden him with the fact that my medication only lets me keep the bad memories inside my head. It's like all my life has been nothing but bad memories, and maybe it's the truth. But I cannot relive the past over and over again.

My darling girl, I have so many regrets. Too many to count. One of them is not being able to experience the joy of seeing you grow up to become the wonderful woman I know you are now. To graduate. To fall in love. To start a family. Maybe even meet your half-brother.

I'm sorry that I cannot help myself, make a small change, no matter how hard, just for you. I'm sorry that I have to do what I'm about to do. I'm sorry that I have to leave you.

In spite of my weakness, I can tell you in all honesty that I'm proud of you as my child. I've always felt blessed to have you. You grew up so fast. Too fast. When I look at you, I see your father. You're just as beautiful. But everything you have, everything you are, is because of me, your mother. Don't cry as you read this letter. I have made peace with my life. I made peace a long time ago and have accepted things as they are.

Both the past and the future.

Even though I'm not with you right now, even though I cannot hold you and kiss you, please know that my heart will always be with you. Always. You're my precious daughter. Ever since the day you were born, I promised to you I would do anything to protect you, to make sure they would not take you away from me, too.

When you read this letter, I know that my life has passed and that my wishes were fulfilled. I went to great lengths to make sure that they were, so when you read this, I know my duty as your mother was well done and that I can be proud of you, of myself, of everything we are.

The past might hold us, capture us, separate us in our minds, but these words will remain. And so will your presence and your future...it's all within our control. Do not focus on the past. Remember me for the smiles we gifted each other and the moments we shared. I love you. Nothing can stop me from loving you no matter where I am. Even though our time together was short, I'm grateful for the moments we had. When you miss me, you'll find me in your blood, in the beat of your heart, in the fact that I gave life to you.

Remember me for who I was.

Your mother

Chapter 24

"SURPRISE," JUDE YELLED the moment I opened the door to our apartment. Behind her were a few of my college friends, neighbors and other people I knew holding a banner that read 'Welcome home'. A huge chocolate cake with the inscription 'Happy Belated Birthday' beckoned to me from a table set up in the corner.

"Oh, my God, Jude," I mumbled as she dashed for me with a shriek. Her arms went around me, pressing me to her chest so hard I had no choice but to drop my suitcases and give in.

I closed my eyes. Tears gathered in my eyes as her familiar scent hit my nostrils. In spite of her overprotectiveness and her tendency to make my business her own, she was the most amazing friend anyone could have.

"Welcome home, Laurie." Alice, Jude's sister, drew me in into a tight hug, too. "Jude's told us everything about your disaster."

"And by disaster you mean…" I shot Jude a glare.

"Chase," Alice replied.

'You told her?" I asked Jude.

"Not just her. She told us all," someone from the crowd. It was Janice, our neighbor. I frowned as I stared at all the familiar faces.

Did Jude invite the whole neighborhood?

My gaze swept over the crowd to take everyone in. Half of them were unfamiliar faces. But then was it really such a surprise?

Jude had always proclaimed that I deserved a big party for my twenty third birthday, not least to celebrate the fact that I'd receive my mother's letters. I never believed her because I never thought it'd happen, but she had been right. *She* had made it happen.

I stared at her in admiration.

Jude shrugged. "I felt like I needed moral support."

I laughed. "Moral support?"

"Yeah, you know, it was pretty hard to see your best friend falling in love for the first time and then realize she had been used."

"Which is why we've declared war. We're going to make

his life a living hell," Alice chimed in.

"You can count on us," one of my neighbors said. "Give us his phone number and we'll make sure he gets the prank calls of his life."

"Oh, God." Laughing, I shook my head as I took the offered drink out of Alice's hands. "Chase isn't after the money. He's actually trying to help me."

"He is?" Jude frowned and everyone grew silent.

"And you're not saying that because you're under duress?" Alice asked.

"What?" I laughed again, then shook my head. "No."

"So you guys worked everything out?" Jude asked. She sounded so sceptical I had to shake my head again.

"No way." I noticed how thin my voice sounded. "We're actually getting a divorce." I plastered a fake smile on my lips that I knew wouldn't fool most people, and definitely not Jude. I expected to feel relief at the thought of Chase and me being over once and for all, but deep down, my heart lurched as realization dawned on me.

I wasn't going to see him again.

Jude didn't buy my smile, as expected. She knew me too well, or maybe she was too perceptive for her own good. With a sense of impending doom, I watched as she grabbed a spoon from a nearby table and knocked it against her wine glass.

"Okay, guys," she yelled, even though you could

probably hear her voice from the street outside. "Would you mind giving us a few minutes? Or better yet, let's meet at Freddy's where the party's starting. Woohoo." She winked at me and ushered everyone out the door.

Eventually, it was just Jude and I. The moment the door closed behind the last visitor, she drew me into a tight hug again.

"I missed you," she whispered, wiping a tear from her face. "I thought you said you'd be back home the day after our conversation."

"I couldn't, Jude." I let out a shaky breath, ready to drop the bomb. "I read the letters."

"Oh." Her eyes fell on the pendant I wore around my neck. "Isn't that your mom's?"

I nodded. "Chase gave it back. You were right. He had it repaired."

Her frown deepened.

"What's going on with you two?" she said. "What happened? Why couldn't you tell me, Laurie?" Her eyes were soft, but there was that glint of accusation that always appeared when she suspected me of keeping secrets from her.

I shook my head just as the tears I had been holding in began to stream down my face. "My mom." I looked up and saw the compassion in her eyes. "Chase brought me her letters."

"What did they say?" Jude's voice was feeble, her face pale.

I closed my eyes. "Chase was right. Her last Will was inside. She wanted me to have the estate."

"That's awesome." Her lips curved into a smile.

"I don't know," I whispered.

"What do you mean?"

"Just that I'm not sure. She said a lot of things. I feel so confused."

"Is that the reason why you didn't come home?" Jude asked.

"Yes." I plopped down on the sofa. Jude sat down next to me, the party forgotten. "I needed time to think, to process."

It was the truth.

After reading my mom's letter I had decided to stay in Acapulco for another week. The time alone had done me good. It had helped me process. Helped me come to terms with the past.

Chase Wright was another story. That was one chapter of my life I didn't seem able to close. Now that he had obtained the letters for me would forever tie him to me. He had helped me, just like he had promised. The gratitude I felt for him would continue to feed the guilt I felt at not helping him get rid of the demons of his past.

"It's not just about your mom, is it?" Jude remarked

softly.

I nodded. "My father's still alive."

"I can't believe it," Jude said shocked.

I shook my head grimly. "Me neither."

"Then, why are you crying?"

"I don't know." I wiped my hand over my face. "A few years before my mom had me she had a boy. She gave him up for adoption. Chase has a brother who's adopted. He has the same first name as mentioned in my mom's letter. It's such an unusual name—" I took a deep breath and let it out slowly, unable to finish the thought that had kept my mind occupied.

Jude stared at me, her confusion etched on her face. "I don't understand. You think he is—"

I nodded. "It's just a hunch, but—" I let out another breath. "Maybe it's just a coincidence, but I believe he might be my brother. But that's not even the worst."

Squeezing her hand, I told her everything. About the rape, my father, my mom's illness. The struggles and the mistrust.

Jude listened intently, her face pale, her eyes shimmering with tears. Every now and then a tear rolled down her cheek. She wiped at it silently, her eyes never leaving me.

"You don't always have to assume the worst, you know," she whispered as soon as I had finished. "Like you said, it's just a hunch. You could be wrong."

"You're right. I thought that, too. The problem is—" I closed my eyes for a moment. "—Kade does kind of look like my mother, but more than that, he looks like a younger version of my grandfather. I didn't see the resemblance at first, but the way he moved, the way he talked, the way he smiled—the resemblance is uncanny." My voice began to shake. "If he's my brother, I don't know what to do. What do you think?"

Her grip on my hand tightened. "We need to find out and then we'll take it from there."

"I'm so scared," I whispered. "I'm so scared that I might not be wrong."

"Let's worry about that later," Jude said determined. "Have you told Chase?"

I shook my head. "I don't think that's a good idea."

"You should."

"I can't," I whispered. "I told him not to contact me ever again. I can't break my own rule."

***

The letter arrived eight weeks later. It looked like any other letter. What caught my attention was the sender's return address. That's why I waited for Jude to get back from work before opening it.

"It came," I shouted as soon as the door closed behind

her.

"What came?" She dropped her handbag on the floor and turned to stare at me.

I held the letter in front of her. Her facial expression instantly changed from nonchalant to anxious. "Oh. What does it say?"

"I didn't have the stomach to open it yet. I waited for you for like four hours."

"Good," she said and headed for the kitchen. "Let me grab a bottle. I have a feeling we'll need lots of alcohol."

"Thought of it already." I pointed at the bottle of wine and the two glasses on the table.

We sat down at the kitchen table. For a while, we remained silent, until Jude pointed at the letter in my hands.

"If you don't open it this instant, I swear to God I will."

My gaze moved from the letter to her impatient face, my heart beating too fast. Groaning, she yanked the letter out of my hands and tore it open.

"What does it say?" I asked and inched forward to peer over her shoulder.

She shrugged, and disappointment flashed across her face. "They talk about confidentiality and blah, blah, blah. In short, they don't want to tell you. You have to contact Chase, tell him about it."

My stomach felt as though someone had just pulled a rug from beneath my feet.

"I can't. I told him—"

"I know what you said, Laurie. You've only recalled that story about a million times." Jude rolled her eyes the way she always did when she was about to lose her patience with me. "But if you don't contact him, I don't know who else could help. Let's face it." She tossed the letter onto the table and interlinked her fingers. "Chase is close to his brother. It would be easy for him to persuade Kade to get tested to find out if there's any chance you guys are related. Don't you think you deserve to know the truth?"

I nodded. "I do, but what if he doesn't want to know? What if we're wrong? That would be so awkward."

"Is that better than living in the dark?"

"No," I said. She was right, as usual. My hands grew clammy at the thought of calling Chase, maybe even seeing him again. "What do I even say?"

"Tell him the truth, Laurie." Jude smiled softly. "The way I see it, you both have a lot in common. You both have lost a lot in your lives. Chase lost his mom to an illness, so did you. So did Kade. Talk to him. Explain it. See what happens. Maybe you'll be surprised."

My heart slammed into my ribs.

At last, I gave a sigh. "I'll think about it."

"No, don't think," Jude said, her tone betraying her annoyance. "Just do it."

That evening, after Jude went to bed, I opened my

laptop. Even though the prospect of contacting Chase was terrifying, it also made me hopeful.

I had to do it.

More than two months had passed since that day on the beach. The only contact we had was me sending him a copy of my mom's last Will to help him with his case. Because truth be told, while Clint might have cared for my mom during their marriage, she had been right in her letters. He had been after her money. By now, I knew her words by heart. She had wanted me to have Waterfront Shore, not just a quarter of the money.

After downing a glass of wine to help me man up, I started to type an email because, even if I wanted to, I couldn't see him. I couldn't talk with him face to face just yet. His memory was too strong, my pain too raw.

It took me hours to write up the parts of my mom's story that were of importance to him: a bit of her life, the adoption, adding my plea to get his brother tested so we'd find out whether Kade and I were related.

Outside, night had fallen. A glance at my watch revealed it was three a.m. Once done, I leaned back and pressed my glass against my hot cheek, welcoming the cool sensation on my skin. I had logged off and almost switched off my laptop when Chase's reply came by text.

You can always count on me. I'm going to ask him tomorrow.

I smiled, oblivious to the fact that he was still awake, and then I typed back a reply.

Thank you. When do you want to meet?

His answer came quickly.

The correct question is where? I'll be at Club 69 tomorrow 11 p.m. sharp.

I stared at the screen, my chest heaving with excitement, until my eyes fell on

Club 69?

69? Is that some kind of joke?

My fingers drummed on the table impatiently.

No joke. It's my favorite.

The club or the position?

I laughed the way I hadn't laughed in a long time.

Was it a wise idea to see him? Could I do it? And 11 p.m.? Then again, the late hour wasn't a surprise. Chase was a lawyer who probably worked late.

And it wasn't like we were going on a date. Before I could reply, my phone beeped again.

Is it true? You really think Kade could be your half-brother?

I bit my lip as I pondered my answer. Then I wrote:

I wouldn't ask you to do this if I wasn't sure.

A minute passed. Then another. At last he replied.

I'll be emailing you the address of a friend of mine who's a doctor. Make sure to visit him tomorrow. He'll tell you how the DNA test works.

I typed my next message, then got up to get ready for bed.

Thanks, I owe you one.

I left the phone on the nightstand and switched off the lights. A few moments later, the screen lit up with a reply.

Do you miss me?

I stared at his text, my heart pounding hard as my brain

began to try to interpret the motivation behind his question. Was he still thinking about us? Was he missing me? What the fuck could I possibly reply to that without offending him, or letting my guard down?

At last, I decided to stick to the truth as I replied,

Yes.

Chapter 25

CLUB 69 WAS one of the most prestigious nightclubs in Los Angeles with similar establishments in NYC and major cities in the United States. That's where the celebrities hung out, where scandals took place, and a long line of paparazzi waited day and night to take that one major picture that would make them rich. Unsurprisingly, it was a place I didn't frequent. The fact that Chase did, rendered me both impressed and pissed beyond my wildest dreams.

The moment I stated my name, the bouncer opened the doors and motioned me inside. I stopped in the doorway to gawk. Boy, was it big and sparkling, with loud music, stunning light work, and exquisite decorations on various levels. Gorgeous women seemed to stand around at every corner, their hungry eyes scanning the crowd for what I assumed where celebrities or someone at least half-famous to hang on to for the night.

Dressed in a short but inconspicuous black dress, I wriggled passed the crowd swaying to the music blaring in the background.

How the fuck was I supposed to find my way to the bar? I considered stopping a scantily-clad woman to ask for directions, then decided against it. By the time I found the bar, I was fifteen minutes late and sure Chase had probably bolted figuring I was a no-show.

As soon as my eyes fell on him, my breath caught in my throat.

He looked so darn sexy.

Sexier than in my naughtiest thoughts.

He was so gorgeous, it took my breath away.

Judging from the tailored business suit and the leather briefcase occupying the seat next to him, he looked like he had worked late. And maybe he had. He was so engrossed in his drink, I had a few moments to take him all in before he felt my stare on him and turned.

His eyes swept over the crowd, focused on the entrance for a few moments, and then they found me.

His expression relaxed a little, and a smile lit his lips as he waved at me.

I headed for him, barely able to contain my own smile.

"Hi Laurie." He stood and leaned in to kiss my cheek. His lips brushed my skin, sending jolts of pleasure through my body.

"Chase," I whispered, my mouth opening and closing as I struggled for words.

"I got us a table." His hand moved to the small of my back as he guided me through the crowd to an upper level where the noise level was bearable and everything seemed more relaxed.

"How are you doing?" he asked as soon as I had sat down and he had taken his seat opposite from me.

"I'm great. How are you?"

God, could I sound more breathy?

"Busy but good." He smiled and moistened his lips. His gaze swept over my body, but didn't linger the way it had a few months ago. My heart dropped just a little bit. Had he moved on already? "It's good to see you. You look beautiful."

"Thank you. It's good to see you, too." Heat crept up my body and face. "You look..." My throat closed in.

He looked perfect.

Like a god.

So sexy I wanted to rip his clothes off and make love to him right there and then.

God, I missed running my hands over his body, kissing every inch of him.

"I'm not dressed to fit the crowd," Chase said nonchalantly. "I had a business meeting here an hour ago." As if to emphasize his words, he let his hand run down his business suit. The ring on his finger sparkled in the lights. He noticed my glance and lifted his hand in the air, a soft smile on his lips. "Still married, remember?"

"Yeah. Got to play the part and all." I nodded, swallowing down the sudden lump in my throat. "How's everything going for you?"

"Good. Much better than expected." His expression remained relaxed, as if nothing could faze him. "The guy knows how to put up a fight. I'll have to give him that. But thanks to your mom's last will, he's going to lose. Big time. I know my game."

Of course he did. I wouldn't have expected anything less from Chase Wright.

"How sure are you?"

His lips curled into a show stopping grin. "Very sure. Let's say we could be toasting."

"Can't. I'm very superstitious," I said faintly.

He shrugged. "I'm not. It's a good case."

"Do you need my mom's letters?" I asked even though I hoped he'd say 'no' because I wasn't ready to disclose the dark parts of her yet.

He cocked his head to the side and regarded me interested. "Why are you asking? Do you have them with you?"

"Just one. It's the one I think you should read." My hands trembled slightly as I picked up the photocopy I had made and passed it to him.

"May I?" He pointed at the piece of paper

"Yeah, go ahead." I shifted uncomfortably in my seat as he started to read.

"I'm going to get us a drink," I mumbled, ready to jump to my feet.

"No need. I already ordered before you arrived."

Like on cue, a woman appeared with a tray and placed our drinks in front of us.

I began to sip my cocktail nervously, my gaze focused on the dance floor below. Club 69 was stunning. Everyone seemed to have such a great time—everyone but me.

At last, Chase leaned back, and his eyes settled on me in silence.

"Why didn't you tell me?" he said softly, pushing the piece of paper toward me.

"I couldn't. It's not something that can be said in an email."

"I get it. It's not something you can discuss." He stared at the piece of paper with a deep frown, his thoughts miles away.

Or maybe that was what I wanted to believe.

"So what do you think?" I asked. "Could it be Kade?

He's the same age and he looks like my mom and my grandfather. If you could convince him to get the test done, then—"

"I already got it."

"What?" My heart lurched. "When?"

I had waited weeks for an answer, and he managed to get the results within twenty-four hours?

He took a deep breath and let it out slowly. "Today. This morning. The results came back a few hours later." He downed his glass before his gaze met mine again.

My body began to tremble with anticipation. My mind was barely able to form the words, and yet I couldn't stand the tension. I had to know.

"What did the test say?"

The silence that followed became unbearable. The seconds that ticked by felt like an eternity.

"He's your brother, Laurie," Chase said slowly.

A gasp escaped my mouth, and I closed my eyes. "Oh, my God."

Kade wasn't just the man who had come up with the plan of deceiving me; he was also my brother.

"Are you sure?" I asked.

"I'm positive. There's barely any doubt." He opened his briefcase and handed me the results. "I wouldn't have thought it, but you're right. Based on the genetic profile you share the same mother."

"What did he say?" I stared at the results, then at Chase.

He shook his head. "Kade doesn't know yet."

I frowned. "How did you get him tested?"

Chase's lips twitched, and for a moment his perfect face reminded me of the seemingly carefree guy from our first meeting. God, he was so beautiful it took my breath away.

"My doctor friend, you know, the one I mentioned, called him to tell him he might have caught a sexually transmitted disease. Kade being the manwhore he is, bought it, so he stopped by the clinic straight away."

I didn't know whether to laugh or be shocked.

Another silence.

"Why didn't you tell him the truth?" I asked.

Chase hesitated. "Look, I'm not trying to sway your decision. It's your call whether you want to tell him or not, but if you ask me, I don't think telling him is a good idea." His fingers clutched at the papers, almost crumbling them. The movement made me nervous. "I've known him most of my life. Kaiden has a lot of anger issues, particularly toward his adoption. In my opinion, he's not ready to face the truth."

"What makes you say that?" I asked

"His anger issues are out of control," he said quietly. "He's a sex addict."

"Oh." I swallowed, embarrassed. "The manwhore part wasn't a joke."

"When Kade turned eighteen, he was offered the opportunity to find out who his real parents were. He decided against it. Instead, he became obsessed with our parents' death." Chase winced, hesitating again as he considered his words carefully. "You need to understand. They had died a few weeks earlier. He loved them. We fought. I stupidly called him a bastard and almost lost him. He actually asked me never to bring up the adoption again."

"Then why did you help me find out?"

"I want you to know the truth, and to be honest, I wanted to know, too." He looked up, his gaze intense. "So, do you want me to tell him? If you do, it's best he hears it from me."

I let the thought sink in for a moment, then shook my head. "Is it wrong that I don't really want to?"

His fingers curled around mine. "No, it's not wrong. You're afraid."

I nodded. "It's all happened so suddenly. To be honest, the idea that I might have a brother shocked me." I searched his gaze and found warmth and understanding in it. "My biological father's alive. I have other siblings, too. I don't even know if I'll ever be ready to meet him."

"Because of what your mom wrote."

I nodded. Waves of anger wafted over me. "He never tried to contact me. He didn't give a shit about her. What kind of man leaves a pregnant woman behind?"

301

"Someone who's not ready."

Maybe. I took a sharp breath. "And yet he has his own family now. His life moves on even though he knows that I exist. All he ever had to do was write me a few lines. Maybe even call. He chose not to." Tears began to cloud my vision. But it wasn't sadness that threatened to choke me. It was anger addressed at a man I had never met. At a man I had no desire to ever meet. "I think I'm ready to move on and forget.

"That won't be possible, Laurie," he whispered. "You need closure. It doesn't have to be now, or tomorrow, but someday, you will have to seek it out. And Kade will need it, too. Just not as long as he's fighting his demons."

"I know." I eyed him. "I don't blame Kade. The last thing I'd want is for him to feel abandoned. But there's a letter my mom wanted him to have. I don't know what to do with it."

"Save it for the right time. Maybe after the trial's over."

"Yeah." I nodded. "How much longer is it going to take?"

"The judge is a friend of mine. The case will be over before the end of summer." His eyes grew distant, and when he spoke, his tone was low. "That's when you'll get your divorce. Just like you wanted." His gaze was tense, an open question. "That's what you want, right, Laurie?"

I bit my lip so hard, I could almost taste the blood. "I

really missed you, Chase," I said instead.

"You don't have to lie," he repeated the words I'd said in Acapulco.

I laughed. "It's the truth."

"So you say." His eyes sparkled, and for a moment there was silence.

He cast his eyes down, avoiding my gaze. I pondered what else to say, how to convey just how I had missed him without giving away the true magnitude of my feelings for him. His gaze met mine, and I realized his expression had changed.

There was a glint in his eyes. The same glint I had glimpsed in Acapulco. My heart lurched as my feelings began to crush me.

"It's been three months," Chase said slowly.

"Yes." I forced myself to smile, but my nerves got the best of me. "Time flies, doesn't it?"

He shook his head. "Sadly, not for me, no." His fingers began to trace circles on my naked arm. The familiar gesture was so erotic, my breath hitched and slow pull settled between my legs. "Are you sure you want the divorce because, you know..." Standing, he retrieved something from his back pocket and pushed it across the table.

I peered at the jewelry box, stunned.

"You still have it?" I asked.

"Yes. I sleep with it next to my pillow." He winked, making it impossible to tell whether he was joking, or not. "Besides, this is worth a fortune."

"Now you're being stingy."

"I know, right?" He winked.

Definitely joking.

I shook my head. "Why, Chase?"

"You know why. I already told you a hundred times. I'll gladly repeat it if you need to hear it again." He smiled gently. "I'm in love with you."

His choice of words rendered me silent. It was no longer 'I'm falling in love with you more and more every day.' It was 'I'm love with you.'

Definite.

Period.

"You really mean that?" I asked, my voice breathy.

He nodded and leaned over the table. His grip on my hand tightened. "I've never been more serious in my life. Indeed, if the situation wasn't so tense, I would have asked you a question."

"What question?"

He slid over, occupying the seat next to mine, and pressed my hand against his heart. "I would have asked you to marry me. In fact, that was the first thought that occurred to me back in the lift, when I thought we were about to die. I wanted to ask you to be my wife."

I leaned back, my gaze connected with his, my mind devoid of thoughts.

When the meaning of his words finally dawned on me, I let out a laugh. "So you admit you thought we were going to die. Because I remember I kept insisting the possibility very much existed, and you kept claiming otherwise."

He grimaced. "Now that it's over, yes, my beautiful wife, I admit you were right. It took a near death situation to make me fall in love with you, but it happened that day."

He had been in love with me from the first day we met? "You're hilarious, Chase." My eyes filled with tears.

"No, I'm not," he said quietly. "In all honesty, Laurie, you're the woman I want in my life. And so…" He opened the box and slid the ring onto my finger. "I'm asking you to stay my wife."

"In a nightclub?" I eyed him, then eyed the beautiful ring on my finger. My heart was racing, my soul was flying—metaphorically speaking, my world was spinning.

"Given that you and I haven't had the most conventional of relationships so far—" He shrugged, leaving the rest unspoken. "Hey, what could possibly go wrong, right?"

"Everything, Chase," I whispered. "Everything."

Like him finding someone else and leaving me. Like both of us deciding we weren't really relationship material.

Or maybe, just maybe, we'd find happiness.

"Hmm," he whispered. "But you've got to admit staying married might not be such a bad idea, particularly since we can't get a divorce just yet. So—" He smiled and before I could blink, he kneeled before me, drawing the attention—and probably envy—of every woman in the vicinity. "Lauren Wright." I giggled at his decision to use his last name. "You're already my wife, so I'm going to skip that part because we've already sorted it out. You've come to me in a desperate plea to seek my help. Now I've got to ask. Are you sure you want to divorce me, even though the sex is pretty mind-blowing, and I'm always happy to offer seafood?"

I laughed, and then I leaned forward and kissed him. "No, I'm not sure."

His brows shot up. "Why? Because you know that I love you, and you love me, too?"

"Yes," I said, sporting the biggest smile of my life. "I love you."

"Yeah, how much?"

"To the moon and back." Our gazes connected, and my heart filled with just a little bit more love for him. "I love you with my soul. And now shut up and just kiss me before you decide to mention crabs."

Epilogue

FIFTEEN MONTHS HAD passed since the case was closed and Chase won the trial, marking the end of my fears, my insecurities. Indeed the end of my life as Laurie Hanson. Sitting with a cup of coffee in my hand and a book in my lap, staring at the sunset out of Chase's penthouse, all sorts of thoughts carried through me.

So many good things had happened since the day I became Lauren Wright.

Jude had made my dream come true by helping me to get a job interview, and I got hired as a marketing assistant to help promote her TV show.

Kade and I had become good friends, but he still didn't know that I was his half-sister. A part of me felt bad, but Chase had been right: Kade wasn't ready for the truth yet.

He had too many issues. Besides, deep down, I was afraid that the delicate friendship slash bond between us would break. But at times, he reminded me so much of my mother, it had become increasingly hard to hide such a secret from him.

His dark brown eyes, his pale face, even his long, thin fingers, they were all painful reminders of her. On some days, I wondered how I could have been so blind as not to notice the startling resemblance.

As it so happened, Kade had an amazing voice, too, and could play the piano, just like Eleanor.

Whenever I looked at him, I saw her. When he played the piano for us, I couldn't help but think just how much my mother would have loved to meet him.

He would have made her proud.

In spite of my initial reservations, Kade had turned out to be a great guy, but he couldn't be more different from Chase.

Or from my father whom I had the pleasure (or displeasure) of meeting once. The encounter had been awkward, and to be honest, I had no idea what my mother ever saw in him. While he promised to stay in touch, deep down I knew that would never happen. Not because he might not try, but because I had no interest in keeping in touch with him whatsoever. Just like Kade, the wounds the past had left behind were too big. Too much time had passed and I just couldn't pretend that nothing had happened.

As for Chase and I?

We were going to be parents any time now. The baby was keeping us both waiting. I kind of looked forward to reading my mom's last letter while, at the same time, I feared the new phase of becoming a mother myself.

Chase, being Chase, made everything easy. He couldn't stop talking about our little family and even bought our first house together, far away from the glitz and the wealth of L.A.

It was an old building he planned to renovate. But the place—in the country—was amazing and oozed charm and a flair that screamed *home*.

As for the estate, it went without saying that we were going to name our daughter after my mother and that one day she was going to inherit my family's estate.

Even though I still hadn't returned to Waterfront Shore.

I just couldn't.

Especially not after finding out about all the bad things that happened to my mom over the course of her life. It was too painful to think that her life had been hell, so we rented it out to a big shot film producer Jude met through work. He had even expressed an interest in purchasing it if we ever decided to sell.

Which I knew we never would.

Clint had moved out, and he and Shannon got married. As far as I knew, they were living in Dallas and were expecting their first child.

I wished them the best of luck, in spite of our fallout after he lost most of my mother's money. I did gift him my grandfather's cars which were worth a fortune.

That made Clint happy.

And it made me happy, because in spite of his greed, I was grateful for how my life had turned out. Without him and his demands, I would never have met Chase, and that was what mattered.

And Chase was perfect in every way.

We were a match made in heaven, even though we couldn't be more different: I, shy and introverted, and he, pushy and always in your face.

He was a good husband, though, and the best lawyer one could get.

I just hoped I'd never have to divorce him because I was sure he'd never let me win, and to be honest, losing sucked.

As I turned my swivel chair to regard him sleeping on the couch—he had been working late again—I felt grateful.

Grateful that he loved me.

Grateful that things had worked out between us.

Honestly, I had never thought it possible, but Chase taught me miracles do exist. After everything that happened, I wouldn't have done things differently.

We married for a reason, but we stayed married for love.

And that's not just a story we'll tell our kids; it's my own personal fairy tale that I hope will never end.

The End

Do you want to know how Kaiden will find out he is Laurie's brother? If you do, join my mailing list here http://eepurl.com/bFUFVT and enjoy the bonus novella "Half Truths" over your morning coffee very soon.

This novella is exclusive to my fans and completely free for all my subscribers!

Watch out for

BEAUTIFUL
DISTRACTION

(A STANDALONE BILLIONAIRE
ROMANCE)

BY J.C. REED

COMING APRIL 12th, 2016

Did you enjoy Bad Boy or Surrender Your Love? If you like a sexy, cocky, bad boy like Chase or Jett (the characters of Bad Boy and Surrender Your Love) get ready for *Beautiful Distraction*.

Kellan Boyd spells trouble, especially when he insists on entering a no strings attached relationship with Ava Cross. This complex man sure knows hot to turn heads and complicate lives. So get ready for another story in which a billionaire knows how to mess with a woman's head.

Coming April 12th, 2016!

Sign up to be notified on release day
http://www.jcreedauthor.com/#!mailing-list/c2egl

One night to remember
By Jackie Steele

What happens when your biggest crush, the one that always ignored you, asks you out, for one night? What if he doesn't even recognize you? Would you say yes?

Coming May 2016!

Sign up to be notified on release day
http://www.jackiesteeleauthor.com/#!subscribe/qejdp

ACKNOWLEDGMENTS

They say no one can do it all alone. And we say that it's true.

Thank you to Larissa Klein for the awesome cover. Thank you to Shannon Wolfman for being superwoman, doing web design, developmental editing, and for making the magic happen. A huge thank you with hugs and kisses goes out to our friend and blogger Kim Bias for proofreading the life out of Bad Boy, and that last minute. You're absolutely awesome, Kim.

Thank you to our beta readers who allowed us to write a better story and for insisting on including our deleted scenes. Your input has been immensely valuable.

And most of all, a huge thank you to all our readers. You are the reason this book exists. Thank you for loving the characters, and for telling us so.

To all the bloggers who've supported us, we want to express our gratitude for helping to spread the word and for reviewing our books.

And last but not least, we want to thank God for all the

little blessings such as giving us the time to read and to write, and allowing books to make our world a better place.

Thank you for reading Bad Boy. We hope you enjoyed it. If you did, please leave a review and spread the word to your friends. If you would like to be notified of new book releases, please join the mailing list at

http://www.jcreedauthor.com/#!mailing-list/c2egl

We might release a book about Kaiden Wright and want to make sure we can notify you when it happens. We also love to hear from you. If you would like to contact us, make sure to follow our social sites.

Jessica & Jackie

ABOUT THE AUTHORS

Jackie S. Steele has lived most of her life in New England. She never read a book she didn't like. Her love for books began when she stumbled upon her mother's secret dash of Harlequin books, and couldn't stop reading until she had finished them all. Today she still loves curling up with a good book, sipping coffee, and taking long walks on the beach.

http://www.facebook.com/AuthorJackieSteele

http://jackiesteele.wix.com/main

J.C. Reed is the multiple New York Times, Wall Street Journal and USA Today bestselling author of SURRENDER YOUR LOVE and NO EXCEPTIONS. She writes steamy contemporary fiction with a touch of mystery. When she's not typing away on her keyboard, forgetting the world around her, she dreams of returning to the beautiful mountains of Wyoming. You can also find her chatting on Facebook with her readers or spending time with her children.

https://www.facebook.com/AuthorJCReed

http://www.jcreedauthor.com

BOOKS BY J.C. REED:

SURRENDER YOUR LOVE
CONQUER YOUR LOVE
TREASURE YOUR LOVE
THE LOVER'S SECRET
THE LOVER'S GAME
THE LOVER'S PROMISE
THE LOVER'S SURRENDER
AN INDECENT PROPOSAL: THE INTERVIEW
AN INDECENT PROPOSAL: THE AGREEMENT
AN INDECENT PROPOSAL; BAD BOY

BOOKS BY JACKIE STEELE:

AN INDECENT PROPOSAL: THE INTERVIEW
AN INDECENT PROPOSAL: THE *AGREEMENT*
AN INDECENT PROPOSAL; BAD BOY